Mistletoe Kisses

A SWEET CHRISTMAS ROMANCE

JESSICA BAKER

CELESTIAL PEN BOOKS

First Edition: July 2024.

ISBN: 978-1-960102-07-2 (paperback)
ISBN: 978-1-960102-06-5 (e-book)

Published 2024 by Celestial Pen Books.

Cover design by Jessica Cobine.

Chapter One

Holly Gardiner stared at the wedding invitation as it sat next to her suitcase. Zoe Bennett had spared no expense with the embossed card stock and shimmering gold lettering. A Christmas wedding in Mistletoe would be beautiful and she was looking forward to it. New England was magical this time of year.

When Zoe called her a few months ago and asked her to be a bridesmaid, Holly couldn't have been happier.

"I'd have you be my maid of honor, like we always talked about, but you can't take off work that long, can you?" Zoe had asked.

Holly had sighed but agreed with Zoe's assumption at the time, because she was busy with work and winter was always busy for photography, what with the photos for Christmas cards, engagements, and winter weddings.

Still, traveling to Mistletoe for her best friend's wedding? It was hardly a hardship.

Holly had grown up there and had gone to school there. She and Zoe both left for the same college, but unlike Holly, Zoe had gone back to Mistletoe, while Holly traveled further south to Charleston to intern at a photography studio. She took over the studio when her mentor Carolyn retired.

It wasn't hard to close the studio for a couple weeks to take a vacation, and she had been looking forward to this for months.

She packed her camera with the intention of taking pictures of the town in winter. She hadn't been back in years, and she didn't want to waste the chance of getting some new pictures for her portfolio. She didn't pack her full kit, just a few lenses and extra batteries. She could already hear Zoe's voice now. "You're coming for my wedding, not to take endless pictures!"

SMALL TOWNS MADE for a picturesque backdrop, even if they weren't Holly's cup of cocoa. The gentle drift of snow looked beautiful in pictures, even if Holly didn't want to deal with it. Growing up in Mistletoe left her mostly immune to the town's charms. She would be lost driving in snow, so being able to walk was definitely a plus.

She hadn't been back since she graduated. Her dad got a job out of state after she finished high school, and she really had little reason to go back. Her family was scattered around the country and most of her friends had moved other places. If it wasn't for Zoe's wedding, she wouldn't have come back.

Her fingers were turning blue from the cold. Changing a lens with gloves made her uncomfortable, so frozen fingers it was. The faster they finished, the happier she'd be.

She snapped a shot and zoomed in, making sure to frame the image so Zoe was just off centered. Her green dress sparkled in the light, and Holly found herself more than a bit amazed that her friend wasn't freezing.

But then again, Zoe had been dreaming about this wedding since the moment Ethan asked her to the eighth-grade dance. She would do anything to make sure this wedding was a success.

"Did you get a close up of my ring?"

Holly bit back a groan. The engagement photos had been done months ago, and the photos Holly was currently taking weren't even the wedding photos. Zoe could have hired a local photographer after her last one quit, but for some reason, she had decided that Holly needed to spend her vacation working. She called barely an hour before Holly left for the airport, which left just enough time for Holly to change her heels out of her luggage with her more sensible work shoes.

"I did, but I can get another."

Holly learned years ago that it was better not to argue with Zoe when she set her mind to something.

The camera clicked several more times, and Holly let out a breath of relief as the battery flashed on the screen for a brief moment and the screen went black. Like her, the camera seemed to hate the cold.

"Battery's dead."

Since she was still a bit discombobulated from traveling, she had forgotten her spare batteries back at the hotel. However, she wasn't about to tell Zoe that. She didn't think Zoe would understand.

Zoe pouted but grabbed her coat off the park bench.

"Cocoa?"

THE BAKERY across the park was crowded for the middle of the day, though with everyone on winter break, that was hardly a surprise. The air inside smelled heavenly, rich and buttery with just a hint of spice. Holly spied chocolate croissants and almond cakes and gingerbread cookies. Steam rose quickly from the espresso machine behind the counter where an apron-clad barista worked efficiently to fill the orders.

"Two hot chocolates," Zoe ordered with a smile. "My treat. Anything else?"

"A gingerbread cookie, please."

The gingerbread had candy eyes and gumdrop buttons and looked almost too cute to eat. Holly traced her fingers over the head. *Why did they make gingerbread human-shaped? Why not make them some other shape so you don't feel bad about eating them?*

She shook her head and took a sip of the hot chocolate. It burned going down, but she welcomed the warmth it brought. It was perfectly sweet and the milk had the right amount of foam. The homemade marshmallows were a nice surprise.

"I know I'm kind of being a pain, but I just want everything to be perfect."

"I know."

Holly offered her a smile, but Holly's smiles felt more strained as the days went by. She couldn't wait until the wedding was over. She was happy for them, even as she couldn't help feeling a pang of something. Not jealousy, not really, but some other uncomfortable emotion that she didn't want to put a name to.

"It's your big day."

She took a sip of hot chocolate and tried to ignore how Zoe beamed.

"What else is left to do?"

"Ethan's parents are taking care of most of it, thankfully. I can't imagine how the rehearsal dinner would be with my parents fighting over who pays."

Zoe's parents had gotten divorced when Zoe was in high school. Her dad was happily remarried, and her mom had a string of boyfriends that always seemed to disappear around the six month mark. For the most part, they got along better now that they were divorced than they ever had when they were married. There were the rare occasions like this though, where they decided to outdo each other.

"There is one thing that you can do for me though."

Zoe grinned slyly and Holly regretted ever asking.

"There's someone I'd love for you to meet."

Chapter Two

NOT FOR THE first time in her life, Holly wished she was better at saying 'no'. Spending her vacation working wasn't enough apparently. No, Zoe had high hopes for this blind date. She had set Holly up with one of Ethan's cousins and Holly hadn't been able to get a word in to protest the set up.

It wasn't like she had anything against him, having met him all of once when she was still in school. Aaron had been a few years older than them, so it wasn't surprising that they hadn't really connected before. Aaron had been on the football team and graduated the year that Holly, Zoe, and Ethan were freshmen. High school Holly had been invisible most of the time, hardly been the type of person that football players dated. Most of them had never even glanced in her direction.

The cafe on Willowbrook wasn't the most ideal spot for a first date. Brunch didn't exactly scream romance. But she was grateful that it was early in the day so she could get it over with and not waste the whole day. Perhaps that was the wrong attitude to go into a date.

"How many?" the hostess asked. Her hair was tied into a ponytail with a scrunchie made of red tinsel and bells that jingled as she walked. It matched the festive decor.

Holly shook her head. "I'm actually meeting someone."

"Oh." She blinked. "Is that him in the back?"

Holly grimaced. She had a vague idea what he looked like, from blurry social media pictures hastily looked up in the back of the taxi on the way over. Zoe withheld the name of the blind date until Holly was in the cab, which was probably just as well since she most likely wouldn't have gone through with it had she known too far in advance she was meeting Aaron.

Even now, she was debating turning back around and seeing if she could walk to town.

Instead, she forced herself further into the cafe.

"Aaron?" she asked as she approached the booth the hostess had indicated. Holly plastered a smile on her face. Where she had at least tried to dress nicely, he had made very little effort. A faded pullover and jeans was not the kind of first impression she expected.

The man looked up and his eyes held zero recognition.

"Oh, you must be Zoe's friend."

"Holly." She held out her hand. "We were a few years apart in school."

He stared blankly at her. "We were? I don't remember you."

She let her hand drop to her side.

He wouldn't remember her. She had seen the girls he had dated back then. Holly was a far cry from his type then, and since he still lived there in Mistletoe, she didn't expect that his type had changed much.

She shuffled out of her coat, just so her hands had something to do beside hanging awkwardly and sat on the bench across from him.

"So, how have you been?"

The words felt funny on her tongue. She hoped they didn't sound too forced, though with the way he was behaving, she doubted he would have noticed.

"I'm doing great."

She blinked. Really? No details at all? Nothing she could work with? He wasn't planning to make this easy for her, was he?

"I'm doing good as well."

He nodded, but his attention wandered back to the menu, lingering on the skillets. She let out a sigh.

"Zoe didn't have a chance to tell me. What do you do?"

He perked up then. So he liked his job.

Holly grinned. She could work with that.

"I coach football at the high school."

Her smile faded.

"Football," she repeated. "Nothing else?"

He shrugged. "Gym, driver's ed, but really, I'm there to take our team to the state championship."

Holly had attended almost every game in high school, but she was definitely not a football fan. For her, attending had less to do with watching the team and more to do with the fact that Zoe went. More than that, Zoe's brother Zach had always been their chaperone, and in high school, Holly had a massive crush on Zach. A crush that had been doomed to go unnoticed since she never worked up the nerve to tell him. After Zach graduated, he had left Mistletoe for college and their paths hadn't crossed offline since. They talked, sometimes messaging until two or three in the morning when they both really ought to be sleeping, but Holly resigned herself to being happy that he hadn't forgotten her when he left town.

"Oh wow," she said when she remembered that Aaron was waiting expectantly for her to answer. "That's very, um, exciting?"

His eyes narrowed. Yeah, she hadn't bought that either.

"You don't have to pretend to be interested."

She smiled sheepishly, feeling her cheeks warm. "Sorry. Sports have never really been my thing." Her fingers traced the edges of the menu. "It's cool though that you got a job doing something you're passionate about."

She was kind of surprised he wasn't doing something more

with it though. From what she remembered, he had gotten a football scholarship, but she hadn't found any reference to it on his social page.

The server stopped at the table, pen and pad at the ready. "Hi. Can I get you something to drink?"

She wore antlers with little flashing lights. Holly couldn't take her eyes off of them. They were just so cheerful, like everything else in the restaurant.

"Oh, I think we're ready to order," Aaron said without bothering to ask before he launched into his order.

Holly was not ready to order. She had barely glanced at the menu, too busy attempting to make this date work for Zoe's sake.

The server turned to her. "And you?"

"Pancakes?" She swallowed. "Chocolate chip pancakes. With bacon, please. And coffee."

The server nodded and jotted it down in her little book. "That'll be right out."

"So..." she said, trying to restart the conversation. "You must find it very fulfilling working with the team."

He made a noise in his throat.

"I know you don't believe that."

"I do."

He shook his head. "You've got that look in your eye. Judging me."

Frankly, Holly didn't think he knew her well enough to know what her judging him looked like. A high school coach was a stable job, plenty of benefits, a retirement plan. If he liked teaching, she thought it was kind of an ideal job for someone who used to play a sport. But the fact that he assumed what she was thinking meant he had probably received plenty of comments that made it seem like he was wasting his talents.

She had received more than her fair share of those comments about photography.

"No wonder you don't have a date to this wedding. Zoe didn't tell me you were such a snob."

Holly let out a squeak. Had she missed some part of this conversation?

"A snob?"

Ok, so perhaps she had certain standards that she liked, but she didn't think it was that unreasonable. She had worked hard for her career.

"Clearly." He motioned at her, from her head to the table. "You came in here looking like that, late, might I add" —she fought back the protests that she had never been late to anything in her life— "and then glare at me like I've done something wrong." He sneered. "No one wears three-hundred-dollar coats in this town."

She bit her tongue. The coat was considerably more than three hundred dollars, but he didn't need to know that. It had lasted her a long time and she didn't feel the need to justify her spending to him.

She would put up with a lot for Zoe, but she wouldn't put up with this.

"I'm sorry to waste your time."

She stood and threw her coat over her arm. His hand gripped her wrist.

"Hey. Where are you going? The food's not even out."

"I'm sure they can box mine to-go." She didn't want to stay another minute in this place.

He scoffed. "What are you going to do? Walk back to town?"

"Yes. I'm leaving."

He stood, blocking her path, and Holly wondered if she could break his grip and run before he caught her again. The situation was sending alarms screaming in her head. Why had she agreed to meet him?

"Is everything alright here?"

Aaron dropped his grip and turned to face the voice.

Holly took her chance to duck around him. Who knew how long it would be before he remembered he was angry with her?

Zach stood between them in the walkway, carrying a plastic

bag stuffed with boxes. The pictures and video chat had done little to highlight how good he looked now.

"Where are you going? I'm not paying for your food."

Zach reached into his pocket and pulled out a twenty. "That should cover it."

He took her hand and gently pulled her away.

Chapter Three

"I APPRECIATE THE RESCUE," Holly said as they walked into the parking lot. Zach hadn't dropped her hand other than to help her into her coat, but he dropped it now to open the door for her. She climbed in and he closed the door before walking around the other side.

He grinned at her. "It's good to see you again. Even if the circumstances are less than ideal."

She laughed. Understatement of the century.

"When did you get in?"

He glanced towards the backseat and grimaced. "Now." He gestured at the cafe. "I stopped to stretch my legs. Figured eating in my room would avoid some of the wedding drama."

He laughed and she couldn't fight the smile.

"I have enough to share, if you want to join me?"

"You're not staying with your dad?"

He made a face. "And make Mom angry? No way."

Holly laughed as he grinned.

He looked good. A green cashmere sweater peeked out from under the heavy wool winter coat. It brought out the brown of his eyes and highlighted the warmth of his skin. His hair had gotten longer from the cropped haircut he had through high school. Not unruly, but just long enough for the hair to fall in soft curls over his forehead and the tips of his ears.

It was strange how despite not seeing him in years, it felt so natural being around him. All the time talking online felt like they hadn't really spent any time apart. If she was being honest with herself, she felt closer to Zach after all these years than Zoe.

She glanced at the bag. "I'm happy to share. It'll give us a chance to catch up in person."

He started the car.

⁂

The TOWN ITSELF WAS SMALL, but there were several inns, bed and breakfasts, and boutique hotels that were scattered throughout. However, the wedding party was all at the same hotel that Holly was staying at. Holly was grateful for it since it meant she could spend more time with Zach without sneaking around.

Holly shuffled foot to foot, holding the food as Zach checked in. They walked into the elevator and Zach pressed the button for the third floor, one floor below Holly's room.

"It's so strange being in the same town as you," Holly said when the elevator stopped, the doors slid open, and they stepped out.

Zach, a marketing specialist, traveled a lot for work, but he was mostly on the West Coast. Even when they managed to be in the same state, coordinating schedules was something of a nightmare.

He chuckled as he unlocked the door to his room. The room was as small as hers, with only a small table, two chairs, a bed, and a small coffee maker next to the electric fireplace. Zach turned the dial on the fireplace and the flames roared to life. Holly set the food on the table. Zach put his luggage at the foot of the bed before he turned to the coffee maker. He poured the contents of the cocoa packets into two mugs and turned on the machine.

"It's nice though."

He set two steaming mugs of cocoa down and sat down across

from her and her heart thumped louder than she expected. The fluttering in her stomach felt like a surprise. After all this time, she didn't think she would react this way to him. When he smiled, she could feel the flush rising in her cheeks.

"How was your flight?" she asked.

Zach reached for the bag and began opening the boxes. The smell of bacon wafted out. Holly couldn't stop herself from grabbing a piece, ignoring how Zach's laughter rang in her ears.

"Long. The drive from the airport wasn't that bad."

She shrugged. "My cab driver tried to get 'lost'."

"You should have driven."

Holly rolled her eyes. "You know I don't drive in snow."

When they were teens, she had refused to get in the driver's seat during the winter months. Zach always found that hysterical but had never forced her to drive. More than once, he had picked her up and taken her places, so she didn't have to. She loved him for that.

"Bacon's not a real meal," he teased, even as he shoved a box with chocolate chip pancakes towards her.

"I can't take your breakfast." She looked down at the box in front of him, filled with an omelet that seemed entirely too healthy for her tastes, and then back at the box he had put in front of her. Chocolate chip pancakes and bacon. "Did you order this for me?"

He smiled.

"How did you know I was going to leave? How long were you watching?"

"Long enough." He shrugged. "I knew Aaron when we were younger. I saw him when I flew in last. He hadn't changed at all."

She shuddered. "I can't believe he's a groomsman."

She wasn't looking forward to seeing him the entire time she was there. And no doubt Zoe would hear Aaron's side of the failed date first. She knew Zoe wouldn't blame her for walking out, but Holly was sure that Zoe would try to set her up with someone else. Taking "no" for an answer was never something Zoe was any good at.

"You know you don't have to go on any of the dates she sets you up on."

Holly glared at him, even as she took a bite of her pancake and swallowed. "You don't know your sister very well if you think I can just say 'no'."

He raised his brow.

"I'm here photographing her wedding, aren't I?'

He shrugged. "Perhaps I just have more practice than you."

"I just need to avoid her for the rest of my life." Holly swooned dramatically. "It's the only real solution."

He laughed loudly, his grin spreading across his face, and Holly couldn't help but smile back.

"I should keep you in my room for the rest of the wedding so she doesn't know where to find you."

"And then kidnap me to the airport."

"You could come with me after. You'd like Portland."

She rolled her eyes and tossed her napkin at him.

"I'm serious, Holls. When's the last time you had an actual vacation? And this doesn't count," he added before she could. He knew her too well.

"I don't remember."

"Then you're due for some time off." He nudged her shoe with his. "Come with me. It'll be fun."

"I'll think about it," she promised.

Going with him sounded like a romantic fantasy come true. But she didn't want to hurt herself like that if she was misreading the situation. A few days would give her the time and space she needed to get clarity and not just make a snap decision.

He smirked, just a hint of his teeth showing between his lips. For a moment, he was a wolf and she was his prey. "I may just have to kidnap you."

"I don't think I'd be too opposed to that."

His fork fell and she smiled to herself. It felt good to be able to take him off guard every once in a while.

"We can't really stay in here all day to avoid your sister," Holly complained, even as Zach seemed more interested in unpacking his suitcase.

Despite her protests, it hadn't stopped her from making herself comfortable. Her coat rested on the back of the chair, her boots had come off, and she was half-laying on his bed. If high school her could only see her now...

"I don't see why not." He looked up at her. "We could put on a movie."

"And I could listen to you complain about it the whole time?"

He grinned. "Just like our streams."

They usually video chatted and played the same movie. Even though they were on opposite sides of the country while watching them, it felt like they were in the same room.

"It does sound nice."

Her phone buzzed yet again with another text that she refused to open.

"How long until Zoe hunts us down? She has to know it was you who rescued me by now."

He shrugged. "It doesn't matter if she does."

He shook his suit out and hung it in the wardrobe.

"Or are you embarrassed to be seen with me?" he teased, and she couldn't help the painfully girlish giggle that escaped her.

"No. Of course not." She tapped her phone screen, watching it light up again. The last message was all exclamation points, except for a single question mark at the end. It had to be a typo where she was texting way too fast, right? It didn't actually mean anything.

"There's probably popcorn downstairs."

Holly made a face. "The bridesmaids are meeting in the lobby in ten minutes."

She was supposed to join them on a scavenger hunt, but she didn't know them very well, at least not anymore. She had drinks with them the other night, made awkward by the fact that the music was so loud in the bar that no one really talked. And despite Zoe's insistence that Holly was her best friend, she wasn't the maid of honor. That was something of a blessing, all things considered, but it was clear that they had drifted apart as they grew older.

Zach held his hand out to her, and she took it, letting him pull her upright. Her knees bumped his legs, and she fought the urge to pull him down beside her instead.

"You're right that we can't hide out here forever."

She made a face. *She didn't want to be right.*

Her phone buzzed again.

"Zoe will be here soon enough," Holly decided. "I wouldn't mind avoiding the wedding part for now."

It wasn't practical long-term, but that would be a problem for the future. Until then...

"How about that movie?"

Chapter Four

THE KNOCKING on the door woke Holly up from where she had fallen asleep on Zach's shoulder. The movie, a cheesy Christmas rom com, had continued playing in the background, and from the looks of the passionate on-screen kiss, it was almost over. The knocking came again, louder this time.

"Zach! Open up!"

Holly winced. She nudged Zach with her shoulder, and he let out a snort, but otherwise didn't move.

"I know you're in there," Zoe's voice came again. "I can hear the TV through the door!"

"Zach," Holly hissed as she shook him again. Her eyes darted to the door as Zoe pounded louder.

He groaned and lifted a hand to his face, rubbing the sleep from his eyes. "What's going on?"

"Zoe's here."

She jumped off the bed and grabbed her coat and boots. There wasn't really anywhere she could hide. The bathroom seemed so obvious. It would be just like Zoe to walk in there to fix her hair the second Zach let her in.

She darted into the wardrobe and pulled the door mostly

closed behind her, barely catching a glimpse of Zach shaking his head at her antics. She heard him open the door.

"Why haven't you been answering your phone?" his sister demanded. "I know you got in *hours* ago."

"I've been asleep."

"Ugh, seriously?"

Holly bit her lip to keep in the snicker. She could practically hear the eye roll in Zoe's voice.

"Give me a break. I'm jet lagged."

Zoe groaned. "Please. You travel more than anyone I've ever met. How could you possibly be jet lagged?"

Considering he had been in Hawaii for a marketing shoot before he went back to Portland, Holly imagined he should have been affected by it. He had jumped about six hours ahead with very little adjustment time. His hours were crazy most days. She couldn't even begin to count the number of times she would write to him first thing in the morning and he hadn't even been to bed yet.

"Never mind that. Have you seen Holly since you abducted her from her date? She's not answering her phone either."

Zach let out a heavy sigh and Holly fought to keep from banging her head into the door. If it opened, she'd never hear the end of it. "Since I did what?"

There was a pause and Holly could only imagine what was going on. She pictured Zoe standing there with her arms crossed, glaring at Zach until he caved.

"I'm pretty sure it's not an abduction if she came willingly. But then again, I'm not a lawyer. You'd have to go ask your fiancé."

"It still doesn't explain why you dragged her from her date."

Holly closed her eyes. She hoped that Zoe would get the hint and leave, but realistically, she knew that wasn't likely.

Someone was shuffling in the room. What was happening? She shifted inside the wardrobe, trying her best to be quiet, until she managed to get a peek through the crack.

"Aaron was being a jerk, like he always is. It's not that surprising that she wanted to leave."

"I know Aaron's a bit much, but don't you think you're being dramatic?" Footsteps passed the wardrobe and Holly held her breath. "Two take out boxes? She was here, wasn't she?"

"So what? That was from hours ago."

"Why does it feel like you're trying to get rid of me?"

Holly closed her eyes and silently screamed.

"Oh. My. Gosh. She's still in here, isn't she?"

"I don't know what you're talking about." The lie was weak and they all knew it.

Footsteps marched onto tile. "You're not fooling anyone. Get out of my way. Holly! Where are you? Come out, come out, wherever you are."

Holly rolled her eyes. Did that actually work? Did people come out and say, 'here I am!' when someone was looking for them?

"I can see your phone," Zoe sang, and Holly winced. She patted her pockets, hoping it was just a trick, that Zoe was just baiting her, but it appeared she wasn't.

The door sung open.

"Aha! Found you!"

Holly blinked against the sudden light. Zoe's triumphant grin shone down on her.

"I knew it! You're here." And then, she blinked. It was like she remembered where she was exactly. "Why are you here?"

"It's not a big deal," Zach said. "We were just hanging out."

Zoe looked at him, then back to Holly, then at Zach again.

"Seriously?"

Zach frowned. "What?"

"Just hanging out?" Zoe squealed. "Oh my gosh! Oh my gosh! Oh my gosh!"

Holly pounced on her as Zoe shrieked. They wrestled a bit as Holly tried to cover her friend's mouth, clearly confirming whatever suspicious Zoe had, and Zoe laughed manically. Zoe finally pushed Holly away. Her cheeks were red, and she had a giant grin on her face.

"I have waited for this to happen for years! Why didn't you tell me?"

"Tell you what?" Zach asked slowly.

Holly glared at her friend, a silent plea for her to shut up. She had never told Zach about her childhood crush on him, and she didn't intend for him to find out because his sister couldn't keep quiet.

"You two are dating!"

He stared.

Silently, Holly screamed.

"I can't believe you didn't tell me." She swatted her brother's arm. "No wonder you went all caveman on her at the cafe. You should have just said you were together."

Zach glanced at Holly. She shrugged.

"It's recent," he said slowly. "Very recent."

"Aww!" Zoe squealed, clapping her hands like a child. She turned her attention to Holly and Holly bit her lip.

"That still doesn't explain why you didn't say anything when I *set you up on a date.*"

"You were just so excited about it?" The lie felt unnatural on her tongue. "And I thought he would be good company and it'd make you happy, so it would have been a nice breakfast?"

Zach shrugged unhelpfully. Holly shot him a glare when Zoe looked away.

Zoe let out an overdramatic sigh. "Fine. I suppose you're off the hook. For now, anyway." She turned, eyes narrowed, and arms crossed. "There will be questions later." Her expression turned wicked. "I guess the two of you would like to catch up."

With that, she walked out of the room.

Holly stared at the door. Surely, it couldn't possibly be over. Any moment, Zoe would come back in and say she was onto them, whatever this was. She blinked and looked at Zach.

"Did we just tell her that we're dating?" High school Holly would have thought she was dreaming.

Zach shrugged again. It seemed like that was the default reaction for the incredibly bizarre situation they had found themselves in.

"We talk almost every day. I'm sure we can fake it easily enough." He smiled. "And it's just for the next week or so."

Holly let out a breath. "Right. We can totally do this."

She wasn't so sure.

Chapter Five

HOLLY WASN'T sure why she expected things to turn awkward between them once she and Zach said they were dating. For some reason, she expected him to kick her out of his room so he could go back to sleep and let her deal with his sister. Instead, he pulled his shoes on.

"I suppose we should probably go mingle."

"We should get our stories straight first."

Zach shrugged. "What's there to get straight?"

"You know." She gestured, as if that would make it any clearer. "How we met? How we started dating? Haven't you ever watched any romance movies?"

He laughed as he stood. "I think they all know how we met. We've been talking to each other online for ages. I travel so much that no one would find it surprising if one of those times I made it by you, you were free, and we met up. Plenty of people have long-distance relationships."

When he put it that way, it did sound like they had been dating. He stopped in front of her, and her heart pounded so loudly against her ribs that she wondered if he could hear it.

"And you've had me watch plenty of romance movies. And I

can't think of a single one where the guy doesn't go along with whatever this is."

She blinked. For a moment, a strange perfect moment, he was so close she thought he might kiss her. She could picture it, him sweeping her into his arms and tucking a strand of hair behind her ear and cradling her face ever so gently as he drew her closer still.

It was a beautiful fantasy.

He didn't draw her closer, but he did take her hand in his and laced their fingers together. His skin was warm to the touch.

"Come on. We should make an appearance downstairs." He grinned, and for a second, it resembled his sister's. "Before they think we ran off and eloped."

The moment was broken and Holly pushed him with her free hand, but she didn't let go of his hand.

HOLLY'S FAMILY wasn't that big. She had been to maybe two weddings as a guest, so most of what she knew about weddings and the festivities surrounding them came from watching movies and working as a photographer. Growing up, her understanding of weddings was about wearing a pretty dress and carrying flowers. Being part of the staff, there was always a certain bit of detachment from the drama.

Her dress had been picked out by the bride to have her blend in, and instead of flowers, she would be carrying a camera. It wasn't exactly the fairytale scenario she imagined as a child, especially not when she and Zoe swore that they'd be each other's maids of honor.

Perhaps she was a little bitter about that. It wasn't like her circle of friends was anywhere near what Zoe's was, though it also didn't look like she'd be getting down the aisle anytime soon to have to worry about it.

With the full schedule of events for the week leading up to the wedding, Zoe was clearly trying to get her money's worth. The cocktail party that evening was just the bride, bridesmaids, the groom, and groomsmen. Tomorrow would be fittings and the welcome dinner. Holly wasn't particularly looking forward to either.

"Remind me again that I love your sister."

He chuckled.

"You love my sister."

The camera felt like an odd companion to the plain green sweater dress. Green, because it wasn't a funeral. Her black dress made her feel so gaunt and serious when she tried it on earlier. Despite it being her favorite, she felt like she was in mourning wearing it.

Mourning her sanity, her mind added helpfully.

"You look beautiful, by the way."

She blushed. Under his gaze, she almost believed it.

"It's nothing much."

If anything, she felt underdressed. At least it helped her blend into the background, which was what she hoped for. It wasn't like she planned to be attending any of these events on Zach's arm.

Holly glanced around the room, dreading seeing Aaron again after that morning, but she didn't see him among the groomsmen.

"He's not here tonight," Zach murmured. "He had to go to a booster club holiday fundraiser and couldn't get out of it."

She looked back at him, wondering how he knew who she was looking for.

"Zach!" one of the bridesmaids called and Holly groaned. Sierra was Zach's ex, though she had been Holly and Zoe's friend first, having been Zoe's college roommate. As far as Holly was aware, Sierra and Zach hadn't talked to each other in years. It didn't stop her from throwing herself at him and wrapping her arms around his neck. "I'm so glad to see you," she said loudly, before dropping her voice lower. "Zoe coerced me into coming tonight."

Zach nodded. "She does that."

She stepped back and smiled at Holly.

"It's great to see you again, Holly."

Holly forced a smile. "You, too."

In truth, she and Sierra had been friends up until a few years ago when they had grown apart. The distance had been something of a factor. Moving away from the area after college had put a strain on most of the friendships she made in Mistletoe. And Holly had never been the most outgoing, social person. That had always been Zoe.

Out of sight, out of mind had killed many of her relationships. She had trouble always being the first person to reach out. It felt like she was imposing herself on them.

Like most people in Mistletoe, Holly had gone to college in Boston. Sierra wasn't from Mistletoe, but she and Holly had several classes together in college. When Sierra and Zach started dating, the distance between Holly and Sierra grew even more.

"How's your photography business going?" Sierra asked, motioning at the camera.

"Really well. And you? Are you still working in marketing?"

It had been what Sierra and Zach had bonded over. Holly had heard all about it from his side, as well as Sierra's. Listening to it from one side was painful, but both sides had been unbearable. The worst part was she wanted them both to be happy, but she couldn't find it in herself to be upset when they broke up.

Sierra nodded. "I am." Her eyes darted to Zach. "We're both adults, right? This doesn't have to be awkward at all."

There was something about her tone that made Holly glance between Sierra and Zach. She never heard that the breakup was bad, but why would it be awkward? And bad enough that Zoe had to force Sierra to come to the party tonight...

"Of course not."

Zach smiled and Sierra relaxed.

"Good. Because I'm really looking forward to hearing how this" —she motioned between Holly and Zach— "happened. But later. I see Amber looking for me."

With that, she darted away. Zach let out a breath.

"First interaction survived. Wasn't so bad, right?"

Holly snorted.

He frowned. "You two used to be close. What happened?"

She shrugged, trying and failing to act casual about it.

He nudged her shoulder playfully. "It wasn't because of me, was it?"

Holly rolled her eyes. It sounded awfully childish to admit that had been a factor in it. "People change." She let out a breath. "Besides, you know me. I was never voted Miss Popularity."

He nodded, his expression suddenly solemn. "You'll have to let me know if I say anything to make you uncomfortable. I don't want us to hurt our friendship."

She fought back a wince as the icy reminder of reality washed over her. She forgot, for a brief moment, that friends were all they were. Especially after Sierra had seen her with Zach and been so ok with it.

"I've never fake dated anyone. I've barely dated anyone for real. I don't know what I'm doing."

"I think that makes two of us." He glanced over her shoulder, then drew her to him. His hands rubbed circles on her back. "Amber is coming over here."

"Of course she is," she groaned.

"Holly!" Amber exclaimed as she bounded up to them. "Zoe told us all about you and Zach. How exciting."

"Leave them be, Amber," Sierra said as she trailed after her.

"But we've waited for this for *years* and it's finally happening."

If Holly was being honest with herself, she didn't think Amber even knew her name before the wedding festivities. They had never been close in school. She was surprised that she even cared enough to remember Zach, since Zach hadn't exactly been part of the in-crowd either. It was part of why they had bonded as kids.

Amber had definitely been one of the popular crowd, right along with Zoe. If Zoe hadn't been her friend growing up and if their dads hadn't been friends, Zoe probably would have left Holly behind in high school.

Usually, it didn't bother her anymore. She didn't think about it most days, and rarely spent so much time reminiscing. But something about being back in Mistletoe was bringing out old memories that she would rather stayed buried.

"I don't know why it didn't happen sooner," Amber carried on as if Sierra hadn't even attempted to intervene. "I mean, everyone totally knew she was into you in high school. She was so obvious about her borderline embarrassing crush."

Holly's face felt more than a bit red. So what if she had a crush years ago? Most people had a crush on someone at some point. The fact that he had been her best friend's brother meant that he was in close proximity and it was only a matter of time before she had felt something.

She could feel Zach staring at her.

"What? Don't tell me you didn't know? She didn't tell you?" Amber laughed, and for a split second, they were back in high school again.

Holly hated her.

Zach laced his fingers with hers. "Of course I knew. But it's good to see you haven't changed at all, Amber."

With that, he guided her away to the bar.

Holly let out a bitter laugh. It seemed like he was always rescuing her from some awful situation with some creep from her past.

She thought that he might ask her about the truth behind Amber's words when they were away from the others. He didn't.

"We don't have to stay if you don't want to. Tomorrow will be long enough as it is."

He tucked a strand of hair behind her ear, letting his hand linger for a few moments longer than necessary, and she knew the others were still watching.

"I'm okay," she said instead.

"No, you're not."

She smiled but it felt like it had been carved with shards of glass. "I can fake that I am." She shook her head and his hand settled on the side of her neck. "I don't know why it gets to me so much. I shouldn't let it get to me. Her, Aaron, they mean nothing to me."

"Because words hurt. It's easy to say they shouldn't have power over you, but it's a lot harder to actually practice." His gaze was tender, and she could have stood there forever, his palm resting still against her skin, and basked in his presence.

She closed her eyes and took a deep breath.

"I'm okay," she repeated.

"If you're sure..."

She nodded.

"If you change your mind, I'll make an excuse for us to go. We could go get ice cream—"

"Zach, it is thirty degrees out there. I'm not eating ice cream."

But it worked. It made her smile so hard that the blush on her cheeks definitely had more to do with the way he was staring at her than it did from Amber's taunting.

"Ice skating then."

She laughed.

"Maybe after tomorrow."

He nodded, his expression serious for a moment as he said, "I'll hold you to that," before it broke into a grin.

Chapter Six

"The dress is stunning," Lauren, the third bridesmaid Holly had never met before that week and who was apparently Zoe's maid of honor, gushed as Zoe gave a twirl on the stand. "It's so perfect for winter."

Holly had to admit Zoe glowed on camera. She looked like a perfect bride. The dress was very wintery and fit the wedding to a tee. It wasn't the princess gown that she always said she wanted though, and Holly found that surprising. Her friend had her dream wedding planned out since they were kids, from the flowers (white roses and baby's breath) to the color scheme (pale mint and ivory) to the cake (vanilla with raspberry filling and cream cheese icing and piped roses). The only alteration to that plan had been the groom, and even that hadn't been a recent change. To pick an entirely different style dress seemed like an omen. Of what, Holly didn't know.

"How many more photos?" the seamstress asked Holly quietly.

Holly felt for them, since they had been putting up with Zoe's whims since she decided she needed to get a dress locally. "I want to support the local economy," Zoe had said, though it seemed like an excuse to fly home several times for dress fittings.

The dress Zoe was wearing now was a far cry from the picture of the dress she'd sent in a text months ago. The number of alterations made her question why her friend hadn't just gotten a different dress.

"A few more shots," Holly promised.

Zoe wanted every moment of the wedding documented. Even the parts that Holly never photographed when working at a wedding. Zoe wasn't mean about it, just demanding. She knew what she wanted and wasn't about to let anyone tell her no.

She raised the camera again and snapped a few more shots.

"We have the bridesmaids' dresses," another employee declared as she rolled a rack out. "Each of them in the bridesmaid's chosen style."

They were all that pale mint color that Zoe adored and all long for the formal church ceremony taking place Saturday, but the tops were all just a bit different. They would look very pretty.

She counted the dresses as the employee pulled them off the rack and handed them to their respective bridesmaid. One, two, three...

"There's an extra."

Sierra, Amber, and Lauren looked at her. Sierra grimaced, her expression more than a bit sympathetic.

"That one's for you," Zoe said as she stepped off the pedestal.

Holly hadn't thought she would be wearing a bridesmaid dress anymore. She was just supposed to be photographing the wedding now, not being part of it, wasn't she?

"Don't worry. I'm paying for it."

That wasn't what she was worried about. She liked to blend in with the audience at weddings. A light-colored dress like that would do the exact opposite of blend in.

"You should go try it on. I guessed your size."

Holly eyed it warily.

"I'll put it in a room," the employee said helpfully.

Holly grimaced. The last thing she wanted was to try on a dress now. Still, she followed the girl to a room. The curtain slipped shut behind her.

She wished she had known Zoe was going to pull this and kicked herself for not realizing she would. She wasn't wearing the right undergarments or shoes for the dress.

She sighed and pulled her clothes off. She hadn't exactly selected her clothes that morning with the intention of trying on anything and she cursed that fact as she sat there unzipping her boots. She brought a dress for the ceremony, a simple, uncomplicated navy blue dress that she could easily move in and had nothing to snag on her equipment.

This dress was the opposite of that, long, snaggable chiffon and not even a pocket to slip a card case and spare batteries in during the ceremony so she wouldn't have to tote a giant camera bag around the entire time.

She slipped the dress over her head.

It looked like frost on grass early in the morning when the first rays of light peeked out from behind the trees and the crystals looked almost like snow. It was a strangely flattering color on her.

The skirt flared out. It was definitely too long and would need to be hemmed, because it was currently pooling around her ankles in soft ripples.

She reached behind her to pull up the zipper, but the placement was just low enough that she couldn't easily reach. She needed to find one of the employees, but she didn't really want to move yet. She hadn't pulled her boots on, not wanting to tempt fate on the chiffon, and didn't really love the idea of going back into the salon with just her socks.

"Holly?" Sierra's voice came from the other side of the curtain, soft enough that the others wouldn't hear her. "May I come in?"

Holly pulled back the curtain.

Sierra blinked. "It's a pretty dress."

Holly snorted.

"Thanks." She motioned to the handful of fabric. "I can't really go anywhere in it."

Sierra grimaced at the boots sitting next to the chair.

"Do you need help zipping it up?"

"Please."

Holly turned and she felt Sierra grip the zipper and pull it up. "It fits you really well. I'm surprised she got the length so wrong."

"She thought I'd wear heels."

And, if she wasn't going to be on her feet all day as the photographer, she would have. The shoes she brought had barely an inch heel and were comfortable to stand in for hours, but dressy enough to go with the dress she brought.

"I bet she brought shoes for you."

Probably uncomfortable ones. Zoe never had very practical tastes. This dress was proof of that.

"I just don't understand the point of this. I'm not part of the wedding party."

"I don't think you have a choice at this point." She shrugged. "Unless you leave town."

"Zoe would never talk to me again if I did that."

Sierra laughed and Holly took in her appearance for the first time. The mint was equally lovely on her, making her skin appear warm and rosy.

"You could hide out in here. Maybe they'll forget."

"Doubtful." But it still made her smile.

"I'll be right back." Sierra ducked through the curtain and appeared a few minutes later. "Ta-da!"

In her hands, she held out a pair of ballet slippers. They were shorter than the shoes she planned to wear, but they were far better than the boots she had.

"They're perfect."

"I figured they had to have something around. You couldn't have been the first girl who didn't have shoes."

It took a bit of maneuvering since she wasn't anywhere near as comfortable in her dress as Sierra was, but she managed to sit down and ruck the skirt up to her knees. They were a little big, but with the thick socks, they would work as a temporary fix.

She smiled up at her. "Thank you."

In that moment, it felt like they have never grown apart. It was nice.

"Holly?" they both heard Zoe calling from the main room.

"Come on." Sierra held out a hand and helped her up.

"Oh, it's beautiful!" Zoe squealed as she saw her. "I knew it would be." She looked back at the seamstress. "You'll be able to alter it in time, right?"

The woman shrugged and moved to circle Holly. "It fits well enough. It's just the length." She tapped her chin and nodded. "I can take care of it shortly, but it will cost extra for a rush."

Zoe waved a hand. "Charge it to me."

Normally, Holly would protest, but since she wasn't being paid for working at this wedding and hadn't asked for a new gown and likely would have no reason to wear a dress like this again, she kept her mouth shut. It was a shame that the dress was wasted on her. It would probably sit in her closet. She would feel too guilty to give it away but had nowhere to wear it.

The seamstress looked at Holly. "I'll start with you to give us time to make changes."

Holly nodded.

WHEN HOLLY GOT BACK to the hotel, she wanted nothing more than to crawl into bed and hide, but if she did that, she wouldn't come back out for the welcome dinner. Instead, she knocked on Zach's hotel door. The door opened almost immediately.

"Bad day?" he asked when he caught the look on her face.

She grimaced. "Your sister ambushed me."

He winced.

"I wouldn't be surprised if I got to the wedding on Saturday and she's hired another photographer and I'm suddenly a bridesmaid."

The words had more of a bite than she intended. She cycled between relieved and hurt that Zoe didn't ask her to be a bridesmaid at the beginning, but she didn't want to be one now. She would be annoyed at this point if she was one, because it would be an afterthought and clearly only because Zoe thought Zach and her were dating. The thought made acid well up in her throat and she swallowed hard.

"She's probably not even thinking about it like that." Zach held up a hand to stop whatever protests she might give. "You know how Zoe is. She's always thrown herself forward without thinking of the consequences. I'm sure in her mind, it's perfectly logical, but…"

He let out a breath. For a second, it looked like he hated himself for whatever he was about to say.

"She hasn't been a very good friend to you. She hasn't been in years."

Holly winced.

"She's my sister and I love her, but she forgets about you when you're not in front of her. Not just you, everyone. Right now, you're shiny and new and in front of her face and she will continue to jerk you around as long as you let her."

"The dress is so pretty," Holly said as she sat down on the bed with a flop, "and I absolutely hate it."

He sat down next to her and took her hand, squeezing it. "So don't wear it."

"Just like that?"

"Just like that."

It seemed too easy.

"You're already doing her a favor by being her photographer. You aren't obligated to wear a dress you hate simply because she bought it for you. You don't owe her anything."

She leaned her head against his shoulder.

"It's her wedding."

"Doesn't matter. It doesn't give her a free pass to be a terrible friend. And I will fight her on it if I have to."

He squeezed her hand again and gave her that breathtaking smile, and her heart thudded loudly again.

"Thank you," she whispered.

Chapter Seven

T HE ROOM at the welcome dinner was loud, excitement buzzing in the air. The dinner was also going to be the first time she saw Aaron after the disastrous date, and Holly wasn't looking forward to it. At the very least, she would have a buffer of other people around, but she didn't want to deal with him.

Resentment, dark and ugly, swirled in her gut. She hadn't been able to say no to Zoe then, and now the thought of seeing Aaron was making her sick to her stomach. He hadn't done anything that could be counted as creepy, not really, but something about him made her stomach twist in knots. Her new goal for the rest of the wedding festivities was to get better at saying 'no', especially to Zoe.

Zach's words from earlier echoed in her ears still. He was right. She kept agreeing to everything out of a sense of loyalty and a tendency to feel guilty if she said 'no' because it felt like she was a bad person for prioritizing herself, and it was hurting her.

The whole fake dating only came about because Zoe made assumptions and neither she nor Zach had been able to tell his sister 'no'.

The more she thought about it all, the angrier she got.

"Have a drink," Sierra said as she approached with two glasses of champagne. She offered one to Holly. "You look like you could use it."

She frowned, before she tried to force herself to smile.

"You look like you're being tortured."

"What did I look like before?"

Sierra shrugged. "Like you were planning to kill someone."

"I don't know about *planning*..."

She took a sip of the champagne, more to have something to do than anything else. Zoe and Ethan had yet to arrive, and Zach was talking to his dad across the room. She wished she knew what they were talking about; Zach seemed unusually animated. His dad had his head tilted and was smiling, so whatever they were talking about couldn't be too bad.

"This is awkward, right?" Sierra asked. "We're all just standing around here waiting. I feel like she did this on purpose."

Holly shrugged. Knowing Zoe, she probably did.

After her earlier revelation and Zach's insight, Holly was analyzing every interaction under the assumption that Zoe was being far more manipulative that she originally thought.

"She practically blackmailed me into being a bridesmaid," Sierra continued. "She totally thought she'd set up the whole thing with Zach and me, and we'd get back together like it was some Christmas movie. Because that's realistic."

Sierra laughed, annoyance bleeding into the sound, and downed the rest of her champagne.

"Zach never gave me the full story on why you guys broke up," Holly said as she ran her fingers along her champagne flute. If she was being honest, she hated the taste of champagne. It was like the wine was spicy, but not in a pleasant way.

Sierra shrugged. "What's there to tell? We weren't well-suited for each other."

"Really?"

They hid it well. They seemed happy at the time.

"We've barely talked at all since. I didn't want to make the week awkward by being part of the wedding party and us being forced to see each other. I wasn't sure how he felt."

Holly glanced at the bubbles in her glass as they sparkled and fizzed. "He never said anything."

"We're too much alike to be any good." She smiled. "I always thought the two of you were better for each other. Seeing the two of you last night... I'm glad the two of you finally figured it out."

Something uncomfortable twisted in her stomach. They were lying to everyone. It was just for a few more days, but it felt like they would do nothing but reap destruction in their wake.

She looked up and, for just a moment, met Zach's eyes across the room. He saw her and smiled, and she hated that he was so good at pretending. It was just going to wreck her heart in the process.

And then the doors opened, and Zoe and Ethan stepped inside.

Chapter Eight

THE WELCOME DINNER felt a little like Zoe had planned out the perfect means of torture. It probably wouldn't feel that way if every little interaction wasn't being painted with Holly's annoyance at Zoe. The food served was rubbery and bland. The room was cold. And to make matters worse, Holly was sitting between to two people she didn't even know. On one side was Zach and Zoe's cousin Noah, who she had met for the first time that night and on the other side, someone she thought might be one of Ethan's uncles. It wasn't like she was even sitting in a good spot to take pictures, though what was she supposed to take pictures of? People eating? People mid-conversation?

She had gotten up at one point and walked around with the camera, but Zoe told her to go socialize because she was spending too much time behind the camera.

"It's supposed to be fun!" Zoe had said. "Go have fun."

No matter what Holly did, she wasn't going to win. It was best not to argue.

Zoe hadn't bothered to change the seating arrangements, so Zach was across the table next to Sierra and Sierra kept making faces and sending her texts beneath the table. The phone buzzed against her thigh, and she wondered if she needed to mute it, especially because Noah kept trying to catch a peak at what she was looking at under the table.

"Something interesting?" he asked.

All that was in the text were emojis. A panting face, kissing emoji, and one laughing with a hand over its mouth. It was just like back in college when Sierra would send a plethora of emojis rather than write something. Only it was worse now, because the emojis were separated by texts with romantic scenarios for Holly to accidentally lock herself with Zach in the coat closet at the front of the building, in the hotel elevator, and even in his room. Sierra offered to track down mistletoe and wine and stock each of these places with them, and all Holly could do was sit there and take it.

"Not really."

He would have been close enough to Holly's type, if Zach hadn't been right there. He seemed nice enough but was also incredibly bland. Part of Holly couldn't help but wonder if that was why Zoe put him there, if she thought Holly was 'nice enough, but bland'. He had grown up a few towns over. She hadn't met him before sitting down beside him.

At the end of the table was Zoe and Zach's great-aunt Victoria, who had become something of an outcast in the family, but Holly always liked her. At eighty-seven, the woman was spunkier than most twenty-year-olds, and she had always been good to Holly. She never acted like Holly was a tag along, not the way Zoe's mom had after the divorce. Victoria had been the one to teach Holly how to knit and had given Holly her late husband's old photography equipment when she first became interested in it. The camera sat on the bookshelf in her condo, but the lenses got a lot of use still.

"There's a Christmas festival tomorrow," Noah said.

Holly nodded. "I saw the signs. I'll probably take some pictures, just for fun."

She and Zach planned to go and drink hot chocolate at the booth that served like ten different flavors in tiny little cups. Maybe they would even get some shopping done. Holly always loved seeing the different craft booths that sold handmade items and it was never too early to buy her gifts for next Christmas.

"You do photography for fun outside of work?"

She always hated how surprised people sounded. Was it a crime that she enjoyed what she did?

"I do."

"Perhaps you'd let me tag along tomorrow? I promise I won't get in your way."

He smiled and she felt like sinking into her seat, especially when Sierra sent three facepalm emojis her way. She had never been very good at rejections.

"Oh, be quiet, Noah," Aunt Victoria said. "Can't you see she's not interested?"

Noah flushed and he sputtered.

HOLLY WISHED she could facepalm without it looking completely weird.

"Sorry," he mumbled as he took a sip of water. "I didn't mean to make you uncomfortable."

Well, that was a switch from Aaron at least. Aaron, who was sitting three seats down and currently hitting on Amber, and it looked like she was fairly receptive to it. It seemed some things never changed.

"It's okay. You seem like a nice guy."

She glanced across the table at Zach. Sierra caught her eye, and when Zach didn't look up, she nudged him in the ribs and pointed across the table to Holly.

SHE HOPED the text didn't seem too desperate and maybe it was a little mean to make Zach's ex follow them on an outing in hopes of taking Noah away. Sierra cocked her head and showed her screen to Zach. Zach paused for a second, lips parting ever so slightly, before he nodded. Sierra looked up and nodded.

"Actually, I'm going with Zach and Sierra, so it's fine if you come with." She smiled at him.

Aunt Victoria snorted and rolled her eyes when Holly looked at her.

"I would really like that."

Holly snorted.

It was weird how it seemed like no time passed between them. It was like all the awkwardness had faded away.

The phone buzzed again, and Holly glanced back down. Zach's name was now next to Sierra's on a new group chat, which

Sierra quickly renamed to "Wedding Survival Group". Holly fought a laugh. Zach had no such issue though and stuck several laughing faces into the chat.

Holly glanced at the woman. Aunt Victoria and Zoe had never gotten along, which was probably why she was exiled down here. Perhaps she had always seen Zoe for exactly what she was.

She wasn't sure what the deal with Noah was, but anyone who didn't have Zoe's favor was probably an alright person. His parents were sitting at the main table with Zoe's mom. Wisely, Zoe's dad and stepmom were not at the same table, so that fight was being delayed for the time being, at least.

Though Sierra was right about one thing. Clearly some drama was happening at the main table. Ethan kept casting glares at his parents and his grandparents. Zoe wasn't looking up, but Holly could see how her jaw was clenched and she was pushing the chicken around on her plate. Something clearly upset them and it was probably the reason why they were late.

Zach said something to Sierra and the other girl grinned. She couldn't hear what it was since the room was too noisy and the other side of the table was too far to hear their soft conversation. A minute later, Zach pushed his chair back and put his napkin on the table before he got up and walked around the table.

He offered a hand to Holly, who blinked at it.

"Let's dance."

She didn't dare say the cliche line of 'but there's no music', because this wasn't a romance movie, and she hated the idea of stating the obvious. Instead, she put her napkin on the table, stood up, and took his hand.

Zach and Sierra clearly planned this in their whispered conversation. From the tiny clutch purse she brought, Sierra produced a speaker.

Zach led her into the open space as the music played softly. Out of the corner of her eye, Holly saw Zach's dad, Dennis, and stepmom, Sharon, stand as well to join them. Even Zoe seemed relieved by the distraction and pulled Ethan out to the floor, though from the tense way they held each other, Holly had to wonder if there was even going to be a wedding come Saturday.

She knew couples fought and weddings were times of tension, but Holly had never been around Zoe and Ethan fighting and never even heard them reference it. They had taken a short break from each other during college, but beyond that, they always seemed so perfect together.

She shook her head. Whatever was happening between the two

of them was not her business. They would either work it out or they wouldn't.

Holly closed her eyes and laid her head on Zach's shoulder as they silently swayed to the Christmas music Sierra had chosen. She could feel his heart beating under her cheek, steady and calm as always.

"I'm done talking about this!" Ethan shouted suddenly.

He let go of Zoe and walked off the floor, barely remembering to grab his jacket on the way out the door. Everyone stared after him.

Holly looked at Zoe, who had gone pale and then red before she muttered "excuse me" and ran out after him. The doors slammed shut behind her.

"Any idea what that's all about?" she asked Zach, who shook his head. He held onto her still.

"Well, no point in staying," Aunt Victoria said.

"Victoria!"

"What? Those two clearly aren't coming back. Food's not that good either. They don't even have dessert on the menu." She shrugged. "I'm too old to waste my life eating boiled chicken."

Out of the corner of her eye, Holly thought she saw Sharon laughing.

"She's right," Zach said. "Let's get out of here."

Chapter Nine

Holly had forgotten the way that downtown Mistletoe at night sparkled during the holiday season. Every store was required to decorate in some way and keep the decorations up through the new year. With most of the town's revenue coming from the tourist population that found it being the perfect destination for Christmas weddings, holiday decorations, and sightseeing the historic houses, it wasn't that much of a wonder they wanted to make it festive.

While she knew that she and Zach were faking their relationship for the benefit of the others at the wedding, it was easy to forget that this was all pretend. Walking beside him on the snowy sidewalk with the Christmas lights twinkling above them, it felt an awful lot like they were on a date.

"Cider or hot chocolate?" he asked as they passed the bakery.

"Cider please."

He held the door open for her and they stepped out of the cold. The air inside smelled slightly sweet, and she watched as they brought a fresh tray of cookies to the counter. Zach ordered while Holly found one of the tables next to the window. He joined her a few moments later carrying two steaming mugs of apple cider and two molasses cookies. The sugar crystals looked like snow dusting the tops.

"So that was exciting, whatever that was," he said as he sat down. "Did she give any indication earlier?"

"None."

He let out a breath.

"I just keep feeling like I missed something."

"You feel guilty," Holly said as she broke off a piece of the cookie. It was warm still and the inside was gooey.

"I feel guilty," he agreed. "It's not my relationship. I didn't do anything to cause this, and I still feel like it's my fault. Like there was something that I missed."

"She's your little sister. It makes sense that you want her to be happy."

"I wonder what they're even fighting about."

He stared into the mug. The steam drifted up and Holly wondered if he could see any answers in it.

"I feel bad about lying to everyone."

He glanced up then and something flickered across his face, too fast for her to recognize.

"We're not really lying. They've all just drawn their own conclusions."

She looked down at the cookie, running her fingers over the edges of the piece.

"Would you still be hanging out with me even if Zoe hadn't assumed we were dating?"

She frowned. "Yes."

"And if everyone didn't think we were dating, would you still be going with me tomorrow to the Christmas fair?"

"Of course I would."

He smiled. "So, it's not really a lie, is it?"

"I suppose not."

For a moment, it looked like he might add something else. He stared at her, lips parted ever so slightly, and Holly felt her breath catch in her throat. She wanted to lean in closer so she could hear whatever it was he might say but the words never came.

Instead, the bell on the door jingled and the moment was over.

He looked away and she couldn't help but feel disappointed.

THE STREETS WERE MORE crowded now than they had been before they stopped at the bakery. People were doing their last-minute Christmas shopping or taking in the lights and holiday displays in the different shop windows. Children raced each other down the street, darting between people's legs. She wished she had her camera, but she was also glad she had entrusted it to Sierra to get it back to the hotel safely rather than have to worry about it.

"I don't really want to go back to the hotel yet. Do you?" Zach asked.

Holly shook her head. "Not yet."

"Should we explore a little?"

The booths for the Christmas festival wouldn't be set up until tomorrow, but the ice-skating rink had been set up for weeks. She glanced over at it.

"You want to go?"

"I haven't been skating in ages," he warned her.

"Neither have I." She grinned. "It'll be fun."

Zach snorted. "Not sure 'fun' is the right word."

"Well, we'll both be totally embarrassing together."

With that, she took his hand and dragged him towards the rink.

THE LAST TIME Holly had set foot inside an ice-skating rink was right before her college graduation. She used to spend so much time in there, using it as her weekly workout, and for a while, she had skated really well. When she was skating, she felt like she was flying. The world around her slowed down until she was floating, the cold air rushing gently across her cheeks.

She didn't know how well she could skate at this point, but she did know that even if she did wind up falling and making a fool of herself, then at least she would be in good company. She might actually be steadier on her feet than Zach.

Holly smiled as she watched him wobble back and forth before giving in and clutching at the ledge.

"It's not so hard. Just like riding a bike."

Zach snorted. "Anyone who says that clearly has never tried to ride a bike after getting out of practice."

"When's the last time you rode a bike?"

"It's been a while. I thought I might when I first moved to Portland. Tried it for a bit, but it wasn't for me." He shrugged and the movement caused him to lose balance. He clutched the railing harder. "Much like this."

She laughed. "You were doing fine."

She reached out to him.

"Just take my hand."

He grabbed her hand like it was his lifeline, his grip tight enough to bruise, but she didn't mind too much.

"It has been really nice spending time together in person," she said softly.

He looked at her for a moment, and she felt him slip before she saw his feet go out from under him. He landed on the ice with a thud and a hiss.

"Zach!" She stared down at him. "Are you okay?"

"Yeah. I don't think anything's bruised. Maybe just my pride."

"Looks like you're falling for me," she said.

Zach's eyes widened and Holly blinked. She could feel the blood rushing to her cheeks as he stared at her.

"Sorry. I don't know why I said that."

She held her hand out to help him up, but his grip was too

strong and when she tried to pull him upright, she wound up tumbling forward onto his chest instead. She landed with a 'oof' from both of them, before Zach chuckled.

"Now you've fallen for me," he whispered in her ear.

"Oh no." She sighed as she pushed herself up. "We've been watching the same movies, haven't we?"

This was a terribly cliche romance movie scene, right down to the dialogue, and she wanted to smack herself for even saying it aloud.

Zach laughed, the sound warm and bright, as he maneuvered them upright on the ice. Holly was regretting her choice of slacks, rather than opting for some warmer leggings, but she had known that falling was a possibility when she suggested skating. *More like a certainty*, her brain corrected. Her knees were wet, and it was going to be so cold when she got outside again. Nothing a boiling hot shower shouldn't fix, but it would still be uncomfortable in the meantime. She could only imagine how Zach would feel, considering he took the brunt of the ice.

When they were back on their feet again, Zach held onto her arm and Holly made sure to go slower this time so they wouldn't have a repeat of before. His grip was a little tighter than she expected, but it was fine. She wouldn't change it for the world.

"This is fun," he said, sounding wholly unconvinced.

She pried his fingers off her arm and took his hands instead.

"What are you doing?" His voice bordered on panic.

"You're so tense. It's supposed to be fun."

She turned so she was skating backwards and facing him. Unlike his words earlier, it really was like riding a bike. The muscle memory came back quickly.

"I'm having fun. I'll have more fun if we just go forward."

She laughed.

"But there's so much more than that."

She pulled him along, having gotten her balance back. She really wanted to get back into the habit of skating more frequently. She wondered if her old ice skates even fit her anymore. Holly made a mental note to check that when she got home.

"I don't know how you're doing that."

Zach glanced down at her feet and began to lose his balance again.

"You just can't look down." She pulled her hand free from his and tilted his chin up instead "As long as you keep your eyes on me, it'll all be okay."

He took a breath and fixed his eyes firmly on her face. It was a little hard to keep calm with him doing so, but she would manage. He was trusting her and she wouldn't let him down.

He kept his eyes on her, and soon, they were gliding across the ice. Zach still stumbled a bit, but nothing like before.

"You're right. This was nice," he said as they stepped off the ice.

"We should go again sometime."

He beamed at her, his smile so wide that for a second, she forgot how to breathe. Holly wondered if he could hear her heart pounding above the Christmas music playing through the speakers. It was hammering so hard it might have leaped from her chest.

"I would like that. A lot." And despite having left the ice, he didn't pull his hand from hers.

The walk back to the hotel was in comfortable silence. She wasn't expecting Zach to walk her to her room, but he pressed the elevator button for the fourth floor where she was staying, instead of the third where his room was. They walked down the hall until they reached her door. Holly reached for the key from her pocket, running her fingers along the edges of the card anxiously. She felt overcome with the need to say something, anything, to wrap up the night, but none of the words that came to mind seemed right. What was she supposed to say to him now?

Zach didn't seem to have that issue though. He leaned in and pressed his lips against her cheek. He lingered there, the warmth from his breath on her skin, the smell of his cologne almost overwhelming.

And then, just like that, the moment was over, and he pulled away.

"I'll see you in the morning."

She swallowed. "I'll see you in the morning."

He waited until she was safely inside her room before she heard him walk away.

Chapter Ten

THE CHRISTMAS FESTIVAL held in downtown Mistletoe every year was easily one of Holly's favorite things about living in Mistletoe as a kid, and she hadn't realized how much she missed it in the time she had been away. There had been very little reason to return there once she moved. All her friends lived elsewhere, her parents lived down south, and her work never brought her back here. If it wasn't for Zoe's wedding, she wasn't sure she would have ever come back.

If she hadn't, Holly wasn't sure when she would have seen Zach in person again. Her face felt hot just thinking about it.

"Good morning, sunshine," Sierra greeted Holly as she stepped out of her room.

Holly hadn't heard that since college, when Zoe and Sierra had the tendency to ambush Holly first thing in the morning. She had never been a morning person and Zach was still on West Coast time, so it made sense to meet up later in the morning for the Christmas festival. Apparently, not everyone felt that way.

"How long have you been standing there?"

Did Sierra really wait outside her door just for the chance to be the first one to greet Holly that morning?

"Not long. You said we'd leave here at nine, so knowing you and Zach, I assumed you meant nine-thirty."

She was right in her assumption, unfortunately.

Sierra held out the camera to Holly. "As promised."

"Thank you."

She checked the batteries, but the charge was mostly full, and it didn't make sense to bring too many spares. She had barely used it last night at the welcome dinner.

"So what time did you get in last night?" Sierra asked with a sly grin. "I never heard you."

"It wasn't that late."

The rink didn't stay open all night and they had left fairly early. At least, Holly thought it was early.

"Oh?"

She blushed.

"With a look like that, I'm going to assume something scandalous happened."

"Nothing scandalous happened."

The elevator dinged and the doors opened.

"Come on, I need details."

"Details on what?" Zach asked and Holly buried her face in her hands.

Sierra grinned at him. "On your date last night."

Zach blinked. "Why? I didn't think exes liked knowing those kinds of things."

Sierra waved a hand. "I was Holly's friend long before I was your ex, and I demand details as to why Holly's face is the color of Santa's suit."

Which did nothing to help Holly stop blushing. It was nice to see that Zach wasn't unaffected by it either.

"It was a nice evening. We had fun."

If looks could kill, Sierra would have struck him down with her glare.

"That is not details." She huffed. "Fine. Keep your secrets, you two."

The elevator reached the ground floor and the doors slid open. Noah was waiting for them in the lobby, holding a tray with takeout cups of what Holly assumed was coffee.

"Everyone sleep well?"

Sierra grinned at him and gave him a playful wink. "I always sleep well."

Noah flushed. When Sierra's attentions weren't directed at Holly or Zach, it was fun to watch the experience. Sierra had often done that during college, acting flirtatious and over the top to get people to underestimate her. It worked too well, most of the time, but it also elicited some interesting reactions from the people on the receiving end of her attention.

"And you?"

"Um, yeah... yes. Definitely. I slept great. Like a baby. Not like a baby. I mean—"

Zach patted his cousin on the back. "Stop while you're ahead."

Noah's eyes grew wide and he grimaced. "Good advice."

"So, now that the lovebirds finally woke up after their late-night expeditions" —Holly and Zach pointedly did not react to that, nor did they look at each other— "we can finally get going. Have you waited long?"

"You told me nine-thirty last night," Noah said. He bore a remarkable resemblance to a deer caught looking in the high beams.

Sierra shot Holly a pointed look. "So I did."

Zach rolled his eyes. "Yes, well, now that we're here, we can go."

She smiled sweetly. "Of course. After you, lovebirds."

<hr>

HOLLY LIFTED the camera to her eye and snapped a few pictures of the garland and tinsel sparkling against the snow. She took a picture of Santa laughing, his cheeks red from the cold, under the white beard. She took another of the elves surrounding him.

She would need to get releases from them before she used their photos for her portfolio, so those may just go up to her social accounts as 'pretty pictures'. She had always enjoyed taking more candid shots than she did posed photos, but somehow, she had wound up taking jobs at weddings and events. Still, she liked being part of that special moment and capturing their happiness. She liked that the photos she took let her clients look back at that simple moment of joy and remember everything they had felt that day.

"Stop taking pictures," Sierra said as she nudged Holly in the back. The camera jerked and she took a very blurry picture of the sidewalk instead. "Live in the moment a little."

"I'm trying to."

Sierra gave her a look.

"I know you. This hasn't been a vacation for you. I'm not even sure you know what a vacation is."

Sierra's expression dared her to argue.

"Put the camera away for a while and enjoy yourself. When's the next time you and Zach will even be in the same town after this weekend?"

Holly winced.

"Exactly. So go make the most of your time together and stop staring through the lens."

It was weird how it felt like they were back in college again. Except this time, Zoe wasn't the glue holding them together. It was nice.

Out of the corner of her eye, Holly caught a glimpse of Zach looking in the window of one of the shops on Main Street. Something had obviously caught his eye and she wondered what it was. With the snow in the background and the way the light high-lighted the bits of red in his dark hair, she couldn't help but raise the camera again.

Sierra came around behind her, her head tilted as she appraised the photo.

"Well, that's one reason to take a picture."

Holly blushed, stammering a little something that may have been a defense for taking it. She knew it was going to end up on her website and she was going to look at it often. She wondered if Zach would make it his profile photo, so she could stare at it every time he messaged her.

Would he still message her after this was all over? He said he didn't want things to be weird between them, and she hoped that wouldn't change. She looked forward to hearing from him, of seeing her phone light up with the notification.

One had been waiting for her when she climbed into bed last night. A simple 'I had a great time. I liked skating with you', but it had meant the world to her. She had fallen asleep with a grin on her face as she hugged the phone to her chest.

"See anything interesting?" Zach asked as he rejoined her and Sierra.

Noah had wandered a bit further down, and she hoped he didn't feel too weird being with them. She didn't want him to feel left out.

"A few things," Holly said, the line ruined by the flush she knew was overtaking her face. She hoped he attributed it to the cold air. She wished she had another reaction to him other than to blush furiously anytime she attempted to flirt with him. Perhaps she would have been able to tell him how she felt all those years ago if she did.

"We should go find Noah?"

Sierra rolled her eyes. "I'll go find Noah. You two should go explore."

Zach opened his mouth to argue, and then seemed to remember that it would do no good.

"How about if we meet up for a late lunch?" he asked instead. "One-thirty-ish? At the cafe over there?"

He pointed to the Silver Bells Cafe at the corner of Main Street. The patio seating was filled today and would be as long as the Christmas festival was open. Most of winter, it was closed because who wanted to eat outside in the cold? But for the festival, they had managed to clear the patio and find some space heaters to make the area nice and warm. It looked like a picturesque place to eat lunch.

Sierra nodded. "Sounds good."

With that, she took off into the crowd, disappearing in a matter of minutes despite the bright red winter coat she wore.

Zach held out his hand. "Shall we?"

Holly grinned. "We shall."

LIVING in the south meant that Holly had little use for snow boots ninety-nine percent of the time. Before this trip, she had unearthed her old snow boots from high school, which had miraculously not dried out completely and were still waterproof, and she was grateful for them, even if they were a bit too big. An extra pair of socks took care of that problem though. Trudging through the slushy piles of snow and mud sounded completely miserable in regular shoes. Her mom had teased her about holding onto things she'd never use again, but in this case, she was glad she had. It would have been kind of silly to buy boots to use for one week.

"Do you see any booths you want to stop at?" Zach asked.

In theory, he could have let go of her hand. No one was paying attention to them, so there was no reason to pretend, but she wasn't going to tell him that. She liked the physical contact. She didn't realize how much she missed that aspect of their friendship until he was thousands of miles away and they weren't able to casually hold hands or fall asleep on each other's shoulders during movie night.

"I thought I'd look for something for my mom. Maybe for her birthday. Unless I find something particularly Christmasy. You know she appreciates this kind of stuff."

Even if her mom liked the crafty, handmade stuff, Holly hoped that she would find something that would be useful. Her mom hated clutter for clutter's sake, so something that her mom could actually use in her day-to-day life would make the gift special and have some real thought put into it. It wasn't like she was planning to get her mom a vacuum cleaner or something like that.

She paused by a booth selling scarves. Some had photographs printed on them, others paintings or postcards. They were pretty, but definitely not something her mom would like.

The next booth had ornaments. She grimaced. Definitely not. Mailing glass ornaments was nerve-racking, but flying with them would be even worse.

"Maybe potholders?"

Holly laughed at Zach's suggestion.

"That's more of an everyday gift, not an event gift."

He shrugged. "A tote bag?"

"Maybe." It would be useful at least.

He held up a tote bag with snowflakes embroidered on it. "What do you think?"

Holly studied it appraisingly. "It's pretty. I'm not sure it's the right gift for me to give my mom *for Christmas* though."

He nodded but glanced at the price tag and dug out his wallet.

"You don't have to get it. I'm sure I'll find something else."

He shook his head. "It'll be my gift to her."

She blinked.

"You don't have to send her a gift."

"It'll be rude to just show up without one, don't you think?"

She turned sharply. "You're coming to *my* family's Christmas?"

His expression stayed blank.

"What about your parents? Your dad doesn't want you to spend Christmas here?"

Zach grimaced. "After the wedding? I think that will be more than enough time spent in each other's presence for one sitting."

He looked down at an embroidered keychain, playing with the ring.

"The offer was still open, right?"

"Of course it is. My parents love you. You know that."

It was an offer she made every year, though only half-serious since she never actually expected him to take her up on that. Holly always invited him to her family's Christmas. However, Zach usually worked right up until the holidays, in an effort to avoid going home after the few consecutive years of disastrous Christmases with his family. Between his parents fighting and his mother's disapproval of everything he did, it was easier to not be there during the holidays.

"If it was just my dad and Sharon, it would be fine. But my mom gets mad when I spend Christmas with them and not her, so it becomes a fight. Especially since Zoe won't be there as a buffer."

Zoe had always been the favorite child, so it wasn't any wonder that he saw her as the buffer between him and his parents.

'Zoe can do no wrong,' he had written once, 'where I can do no right.'

Holly wondered if they still saw it like that after last night.

She squeezed his hand. "I want you to come to my family's Christmas. I wouldn't have invited you if I didn't want you there."

Relief flashed over his face. He had that same look he did last night, like he wanted to tell her something but wasn't sure where to begin. They never had any trouble telling each other things online. Was it just that being in person was so different?

She wanted to ask him. The question burned in her throat. She opened her mouth, preparing to speak when he looked away and Holly swallowed her words.

Chapter Eleven

"Do you mind if we stop by my dad's after this?" Zach asked as they finished shopping.

Noah and Sierra had quickly disappeared after lunch with a brief goodbye, leaving the two of them to their own devices. While Holly knew it was to help with the matchmaking, she wasn't about to complain about having alone time with Zach.

Holly shook her head.

"It's just a quick errand."

"I don't mind going with you," she told him. It was definitely better than going back to the hotel alone.

Zach relaxed, and until that moment, she hadn't realized how tense he was.

"Is everything okay?" she asked, nerves suddenly twisting her stomach.

He offered her a bright smile.

"It's nothing to worry about."

That did little to soothe the worries that had taken root.

Holly always liked the Bennett house. It was the kind of place that suited a Northern town so well, a two-story historical house with fireplaces in nearly every room. It had been in their family for a really long time and Zach's dad had continued living there after the divorce.

Zach climbed the stairs up to the front door and knocked.

"I forgot my key at home," he explained sheepishly.

Holly laughed. It was just like him.

The door opened and Zach's dad Dennis appeared. "Door's unlocked. You could have come right in."

"Dad!" Zach groaned. "That's so unsafe."

"In a town like this? Nah. Everyone would know right away."

It was true. Holly remembered when a senior in her class thought it'd be a good idea to steal the Driver's Ed car to take his girlfriend to prom. Everyone knew by dinner time, and he had been grounded by his parents through graduation before the sheriff could even get to their house.

Zach rolled his eyes. "Still."

It was clearly an old argument.

"Holly!" Dennis exclaimed as he saw her standing behind Zach. "It's good to see you again."

"It's good to see you, too."

He smiled and opened the door wider. "Come in, both of you. It's cold out there. You look like you're freezing, Holly."

She grinned sheepishly. "Just a bit."

"You've gotten too used to living down south."

They stepped inside and Holly let out a breath as he closed the door behind them. The house was nice and warm.

"Let me take your coat?"

"Oh, um?" She glanced back at Zach, who was shrugging off his own coat. "Sure. Thank you."

She turned and let Dennis help her out of the coat. She didn't think they were staying long, but with the way the house smelled of Christmas cookies baking and woodsmoke and pine, it made her want to linger. She took her boots off and put them on the mat next to the door with the other boots. She was glad she was wearing her pretty snowflake-patterned socks that Sharon had sent her last Christmas.

"How have your parents been?" Dennis asked her as he led them inside.

"Good. Dad was talking about coming up here again soon."

"Sharon is in the kitchen, if you want to go in there instead," Dennis said, before he guided Zach off upstairs.

It had been years since she had been in their house, but she didn't think she'd ever forget where everything was. She passed through the living room with the beautifully decorated tree with presents surrounding it and the fire crackling in the fireplace. Holly lingered there, holding her hands out in front of the flames to warm her fingers. It felt so nice to stand in front of a proper fire again, and she could have stayed there all day.

"Holly?" Sharon asked as she popped her head out from the kitchen. She wore a holiday apron over an impressively ugly Christmas sweater. A bright red candy cane headband stood out in her almost white hair. "I thought I heard you and Zach."

"Yeah, he's upstairs with his dad."

"Do you want to help me in the kitchen? I just put the last tray in the oven. The ones that have cooled can be decorated."

Holly smiled. "I'd love to help."

Sharon was a great baker and Holly loved Sharon's cookies, even though she hadn't had them in years.

Frosting in piping bags and little bowls of sprinkles sat on the counter near the rack where the cookies were cooling. It would be easier to decorate them when they were cool.

Decorating cookies wasn't an adequate distraction from wondering what Zach was doing upstairs. It wasn't like him to be so secretive, but despite being in the same town as him, she almost felt further away from him than when they were separated by a computer screen. Her fingers itched to write to him and ask him what was wrong, but she was afraid that he would say nothing.

The knot of worry that had formed in her stomach, the one

that said she messed things up between them by not making it clear to Zoe that they weren't dating, tightened.

"Is everything okay?" Sharon asked.

Holly smiled and hoped it didn't look too fake. "Just trying to figure out what would look best."

"If that's all," she said, but sounded unconvinced. "I'm happy to talk if you need it."

Holly didn't think Sharon really wanted to hear about her potential relationship troubles. She also wouldn't dare start venting when Zach might come downstairs at any second and would accidentally overhear her. She didn't want him to misunderstand anything that she said, which there was a chance that would happen if he overheard something out of context.

It seemed he was summoned by the thought. She could hear footsteps as he and his dad came down the stairs and walked into the kitchen.

"How's the decorating coming?" Dennis asked them as he stepped into the doorway.

Sharon smiled.

"Stay. Eat some cookies. It's hardly fair to put in all that work and not enjoy them."

Holly hesitated, but Zach smiled and nodded. "Cookies sound great."

———

THE LIVING ROOM was warm and cozy, especially with the fire going. Holly curled up against the arm of the sofa, as she waited for Sharon to join them. Neither Zach nor his dad said what exactly Zach was there about or why the errand was a secret. It only made her more curious.

Despite the weird emotional distance, Zach was physically close to her. If she turned slightly, she would be curled up against his chest instead of the couch. If his arm had been wrapped around her shoulders, they would be cuddling. Instead, her hand was in his as he played with her fingers, tracing patterns on the chipped nail polish she had left only because Zoe said they would all be getting manicures the morning before the wedding.

"I was cleaning the other day and look what I found!" Sharon said as she sat down. She put the photo album in Zach's lap so they could all look. Holly didn't even know anyone still kept photo albums. Their mom, Amanda, didn't seem like the type to make them. "It's you and Zoe playing brides."

Holly recognized herself wearing the veil and a dress much too long for her. Zach, by default of being the only boy there at the time, had been the groom. Even back then, Zoe liked to match-make, it seemed.

He was holding her hand in most of the photos, much like he was now as they sat on the couch. They had always been that way, holding hands and hugging and touching often. It wasn't really a wonder why people bought their lie so easily.

She wasn't prepared for the picture of Zach kissing her. He hadn't been either, from the way he tensed, and his hand clenched hers tighter.

On the next page, Holly saw herself as an awkward middle schooler. She hadn't had a date to the eighth-grade dance, but the Bennetts had been her ride, so she was standing off to the side, arm wrapped across her middle as Ethan and Zoe posed in the center of the frame, completely oblivious. It was an uncomfortable window into her feelings back then, how alone she felt even as she had forced a misshapen smile on her face to try to pretend she was happy. After that night, it was always Zoe *and* Ethan.

The next photo was from the same night. She wasn't sure it was even supposed to have been taken. She remembered the moment, oddly enough. Her barrette had slipped out and Zach had stepped in to fix it. His hand had been on her cheek and he had been looking down at her so tenderly. She had thought he was so perfect that night, mostly because he had been so kind to her. Up until then, he had just been Zoe's annoying older brother.

She squeezed his hand tighter and smiled up at him.

"You looked really pretty that night," he said softly. "I always wondered why you didn't have a date for that dance."

She shrugged. "I wasn't really interested, I guess. I just wanted to go to have fun with my friends."

Zoe hadn't been her only friend in middle school, but she had definitely been her closest. She spent a lot of time dancing as a group, but none of the boys her age really caught her eye.

She had wound up skipping most of the high school dances. The girls had gotten crueler by that age, and it was easier and cheaper to skip them. She never regretted not going to prom, though she would have liked to wear a pretty dress and dance with someone she liked, but that wasn't going to happen in high school anyway. In high school, she had been too obsessed with getting good grades and focused on the future to be attractive to any of the guys in her class. She wasn't sure she would have gone out with them anyway, just because she didn't want to be stuck in a small town the rest of her life.

She might have made an exception for Zach, but even then, she wasn't sure if she would have. Maybe just for that one night, but until he moved away, she thought for sure that he was going to stay in Mistletoe forever.

Holly hadn't dated until she went to college. While she liked the guys she had gone out with during college and after that, none of them had been right. Her break-ups never evoked the kind of emotion she heard about in songs or saw in movies or read about in books. She never felt like her life was over because they were out of her life or that she'd never move forward and be happy again. The only one she had ever felt that strongly about was sitting beside her on the couch now.

The photo album was mostly empty after high school, with the exception of a family Christmas photo.

"It'll be nice to have some new photos to put in here," Sharon said.

Holly blinked. "You still update it? Even though you can do online albums?"

She smiled. "Do you still take pictures on film?"

Holly shrugged. Not frequently. It was a pain to get developed and she didn't have the facilities to develop it herself. She always wanted a dark room of her own, but outside of the art of it, there really wasn't much call for it. She never had a class on how to develop film, since everything was mostly digital by the time she got into photography, and she hated that it felt like a lost art.

"Only for fun."

Sharon smiled as she stood. "Well, you two will have to take one together while you're here in Mistletoe. It'll be nice to have one of the two of you all grown up."

Zach's cheeks were a little red as he looked down at the page. His fingers traced over the photo of them in high school. There was something about his expression that was odd. She wanted to ask him about it but didn't want to ask in front of his parents. Instead, she shifted closer and leaned her head on his shoulder. Whatever it was, he would tell her when he was ready.

Chapter Twelve

"Do you think there will even still be a wedding?" Holly asked as they walked to the hotel's bar that evening. Since reconnecting, it felt like Sierra was well on the way to being her new best friend.

Sierra shrugged.

"I think someone would have told us if there wasn't."

It didn't stop Sierra from bouncing over to the bar and ordering two drinks.

"I can't," Holly said. "I haven't really drunk anything stronger than that champagne last night in a while and my tolerance is probably way low and I need to be functional tomorrow."

Sierra snorted. "All the more reason to drink tonight. No one needs to be functional tomorrow."

"Does anyone even know what they're fighting about?"

"Amber and Lauren have some guesses." She leaned in closer, her breath tickling Holly's cheek. "Amber thinks Zoe's pregnant and didn't tell Ethan."

"His reaction doesn't make sense for that."

Sierra shrugged.

"Lauren thinks she took a job and is going to have to move and didn't tell Ethan."

Part of her hated speculating and gossiping. The other part of her was dying to know.

The cocktail Sierra ordered, a fancy Christmas-themed concoction, smelled like sugar and spice, but the alcohol burned on her tongue and the back of her throat. She took another sip, but it didn't help, though the flavor was nice.

"Is this gingerbread?"

Sierra nodded.

"There's a whole holiday-themed drink menu." She grinned. "I want to try them all."

"Not tonight, right?"

Sierra shrugged. "When else are we going to try them? We won't have time the next few days."

Holly winced.

"So, drink up! We're going to have fun tonight."

<hr>

HOLLY WAS ONLY HALFWAY through Sierra's proposed drink list when she stood up, her legs going numb from sitting.

"No!" Sierra cried, gripping Holly's arm a bit tighter than necessary. "You can't go yet."

"I'm not," she promised.

She wasn't sure how far she could go with the way the room was spinning. She felt fine, but also very far from fine.

"I need the bathroom."

"But then you'll leave me and I'll be all alone."

Holly held out her purse. "You can hold this so you know I'll come back."

Sierra sat up and beamed, clapping her hands together before she swung the purse over her head. "I'll guard it with my life."

The bathroom was quiet when she staggered in, tripping on the door ledge and the uneven tiles before she got to the stall door. Holly hated feeling so out of it. She never had gone overboard with drinking and usually drank lots of water at the same time because she always felt so dry and dehydrated after. Her head was already pulsing, and she didn't like it.

As she finished up, the door opened before she could leave the stall. She heard the door lock and someone sob softly.

Holly opened the door and stepped into the main area.

"Are you okay?" she asked aloud, the cocktails making her braver than usual. She felt stupid for even asking it. Who cried in a hotel bathroom if they were okay?

No answer came, so she washed her hands. Through the sound of the faucet, she could hear the muffled sobs again.

Holly frowned as she dried her hands. It didn't seem right to leave someone that upset alone. Even if she didn't know them or couldn't help, she could at least make sure they weren't by themselves. She peeked under the stall, just enough to see that there were definitely feet and she hadn't just imagined the whole thing. Red sparkly sandals... she knew those shoes.

"Zoe?" she asked, knocking on the door. "Are you okay?"

The crying cut off again.

"Holly?"

"Yeah."

She heard shuffling and then the door opened. Zoe looked awful, to put it mildly. Her eyes were red and blotchy, and her makeup was caked where the tears had run.

"What happened?"

"Nothing."

But she refused to look up.

"Clearly it's not nothing."

Zoe looked up at her for a half a second before she burst into tears again. Holly reached out and hugged her. No matter how annoyed she was at Zoe, no one deserved to be alone through this.

"What happened?" Holly asked again.

"No one tells me anything," she sobbed into Holly's shoulder. "Mom didn't tell me that she's moving. You and Zach didn't tell me about you two being together. And Ethan—"

She cut herself off.

Dread curdled in Holly's gut. "Ethan what?"

Zoe swallowed hard, the words catching in her throat as she spoke, "Ethan's deploying."

Holly blinked.

"He didn't want to tell me until after the wedding." She rubbed at her eyes. "He said he didn't want to ruin the wedding." Zoe scoffed. "I don't care about that. I just feel like he didn't trust or respect me enough to tell me the truth. How can I marry him if he doesn't think he can be honest with me?"

She tried to recall if she knew Ethan was in the military. Closing her eyes, she remembered seeing a picture of him in uniform, but it was strange that Zoe hadn't really talked about it. Ethan had been in college and had just finished up his doctorate in the spring. It was part of why they were getting married now after being together for so long.

"He didn't tell you he enlisted?" she clarified.

Zoe shook her head.

"He's been enlisted for years. He enlisted when he got his masters. I always knew he would be doing something once he graduated and I was supportive of that. He just didn't tell me that he'd already gotten his orders."

"Oh."

She sniffed and nodded. "We'll have to pack up and move right after the wedding." She rubbed at her face. "I just want this to all be over with so I can go home and start packing."

Holly gave her a squeeze. "It'll be over soon. It's probably a good idea for you to sleep. And wash your face and all."

The words started slurring together, but she didn't care. This explained a lot about Zoe's recent behavior. Her world was spiraling out of control so she wanted to control everything. Holly reached into her pocket and pulled out her phone, quickly texting Sierra.

Found Zoe. Taking her upstairs

SIERRA

Boooooooooooooooo

Holly laughed, despite the inappropriateness of it. Zoe looked up and laughed as she saw Sierra's reply.

"I'm glad you're both getting along again."

"We never weren't getting along. We just grew apart. It happens."

Her answer made Zoe's shoulders slump. Holly shook her head, regretting it when the room began spinning again before her eyes. She wrapped her arm around Zoe, hoping to hide just how affected she was. Leaning against Zoe helped to stabilize her. She could only hope that she didn't smell too much of alcohol. Though Zoe might not have even noticed because she smelled the same.

"Let's get you upstairs," she said. "You should get some sleep."

Zoe nodded. She didn't seem to realize that she was holding Holly upright, because she leaned her head onto Holly's shoulder and snuggled against her as they walked to the elevator.

"I hate that we've grown apart," Zoe whispered as the doors closed. "We used to tell each other everything."

Holly grimaced. She didn't think that Zoe even noticed or cared.

"If I had known you were dating Zach, I'd have asked you instead of Sierra to be a bridesmaid. I didn't want the two of you to fight."

Holly flinched. Zoe thought she was being kind, but her words felt as sharp as knives. Holly thought they had been better friends than that.

Worse was she didn't think that Holly would be mature enough to not fight with someone who used to be her friend. Zoe really thought that Holly would go out of the way to ruin her wedding. *In vino veritas* and all that.

"I'm sorry I had to choose between you two."

Holly plastered a smile on her face —she noticed she faked a lot of smiles here, far more than she usually did— but doubted Zoe would have even noticed if she was frowning or crying or anything else.

"We're almost there," Holly said instead of an answer. "Do you have your key?"

Zoe blinked and patted down her pockets. She proudly produced a room key, holding it up like it was something much more precious than a piece of plastic.

"Great. Where's your room?"

"It's this way," Zoe said, tears forgotten as she led Holly down the hall to the door. She ran the key along the electric lock and opened the door. "Do you want to come in and watch movies like the old days? I could braid your hair and we can tell each other secrets."

Considering her filter was wearing away quickly, she wasn't sure what she might say if she stayed. Probably something that would piss off Zoe in the morning, if she even remembered. Holly wasn't sure she was drunk enough to forget.

"I just want to go upstairs and go to sleep."

Zoe blinked several times. "Oh. Okay." And then, she smiled as she stepped inside. "See you tomorrow."

The door slammed shut behind her. Holly stared at it for several moments, trying to figure out what exactly had just happened. Was Zoe angry? Had she given the wrong answer? Or maybe Zoe was just really out of it too. It wouldn't be that surprising.

She walked —stumbled really— down the hallway. It was only once she got to the elevator that she realized her purse was still downstairs with Sierra. Her cell phone was in her pocket, so that was one thing at least.

She was already on the third floor. She didn't think he would turn her away. Holly tripped twice and twisted her ankle by the time she knocked on the door. Zach opened it a moment later, wearing a tee shirt and sweatpants.

"Hi," she said, wrapping her arms around him as she stumbled forward. "I'm a little drunk and Sierra has my room key."

He blinked.

"Can I stay here? It's too far to go back downstairs, and I don't want to be alone."

He stepped back, bring her with him. The door swung shut behind him. "Of course you can stay."

"I talked to Zoe." His arms tightened around her. And then, once she started talking, the words came out in a rush. "She's upset everyone's lying to her and apparently Ethan's in the military and stationed somewhere and she never even said he joined anything but she's mad at me that we lied but she doesn't know that we're still lying."

She buried her face in his neck and refused to look up at him again.

"How much exactly did you drink?"

She shook head.

"Sierra kept switching glasses when I finished." She stilled. "Not with hers. With new drinks. She wanted to try the entire Christmas menu."

"I see," Zach said slowly. He did not sound like he did see.

"Sierra has my room key." Had she told him that already? She wasn't sure if she had.

She inhaled. His cologne smelled nice. It wasn't overwhelming, just warm, and she wanted to wrap herself up in the scent forever.

Zach pulled back, unwinding himself from her, and Holly thought she may have whined at the loss.

"That can't be comfortable to sleep in," he said, motioning to her outfit.

He walked over to his suitcase and pulled out a tee shirt, a pair of pajama pants, and socks for her. "Let me know if you need anything else."

"Thanks."

He smiled and Holly thought her heart might beat out of her

chest. The room felt like it was spinning again, even as she fled to the bathroom.

It would be weird to use his toothbrush, she decided, though she did put some of his toothpaste on her finger and rubbed it around her mouth. It was better than going to bed with the taste of alcohol on her tongue.

She washed her face with the bar of soap and a washcloth and was grateful that the waterproof makeup made her eyes itchy, so she hadn't used it.

His pajamas were soft and his tee shirt smelled like him. She was just glad the door was closed so he couldn't see how she lifted the material to her face and inhaled deeply, keeping her eyes shut as she breathed in.

A knock came from the other side of the door and Holly startled, jumping a little.

"Holly? You okay in there?"

She blinked. "Yeah. I'm fine."

She blushed. The little room felt too warm suddenly, especially wearing his clothes and sniffing them. She would never admit to doing it and probably would never do that again. She wasn't in high school after all. She could be mature about spending the night in the same bed with the guy she liked, sleeping in his clothes and probably snuggling him.

Maybe she couldn't.

She looked in the mirror for a moment before she turned on the water and splashed her cheeks. She could do this. There was nothing weird about platonically sharing a bed with someone.

She opened the door before she could overthink it too much.

Zach stood on the other side of the threshold, half-turned and ready to walk away. "Ready?"

She nodded and let him take her hand.

Lying in bed beside him was nice. The bed was cozy and his pajamas were warm. She could easily get used to this, which wouldn't be as fun when he was on the other side of the country.

"Your shoulder is a nice pillow," she murmured sleepily. She thought she heard him say something in return but couldn't quite make it out as she drifted off.

Chapter Thirteen

HOLLY WOKE to an unfortunate throbbing in her head that only worsened as she sat upright. Any other morning, she might have been disappointed that she had fallen asleep with Zach and not woken up beside him, but this morning, she was glad for it. He held out a glass of water and an aspirin.

"That whole saying 'no'? You realize it applies to more than saying no to Zoe, right?"

She groaned but took the offered aspirin. She drank the entire glass of water, so fast she thought she might be sick from it, but she was also so thirsty that she didn't really care.

"I did say no."

He raised his eyebrows at her in disbelief.

"I don't know. This week has just been a lot. I wanted to have fun and not think about the wedding," she corrected herself. She stared down at the glass. "It was fun for a bit."

"Are you going to be okay?"

She nodded. She didn't drink anywhere near what Sierra had. A few more hours of sleep would have been nice, but the clock's red numbers across the room told her that wasn't possible.

"A shower and coffee will do wonders."

But she needed to get into her room. She couldn't just wear his clothes all day and the thought of putting her clothes back on made her want to cringe.

"I can definitely do something about the coffee." He motioned to the little machine on the other side of the room. "You said Sierra had your room key?"

"Yeah."

He nodded sharply and pulled out his phone. He typed something before he moved to the coffee maker. Despite her usually not enjoying hotel coffee, she could smell it across the room. He handed her a mug a few minutes later, lingering so close that, for a moment, she thought he was going to kiss her head. He didn't and she hated that she wanted him to so badly.

His phone buzzed and Zach pulled it out again.

"I'm going to go get your purse from Sierra's room," he said and walked out before she could even say a word.

***

By the time Zach returned, Holly had managed to get her shoes on, as well as gathered her clothes from where she left them on the chair the night before. Between the coffee and the aspirin, she felt no worse than any other early morning.

"I'm sorry if I did anything embarrassing last night." She didn't remember doing anything, but that didn't mean she hadn't forgotten something.

Zach shook his head. "You didn't."

For some reason, she didn't believe him. Something felt off, and it took her a little while to realize it was because he had spent the whole morning avoiding her eyes.

"Did I do something to make you uncomfortable?"

He didn't answer, and it made her stomach twist worse than the alcohol ever could.

"Please," she begged. "I never wanted to make you feel uncomfortable."

Zach let out a breath and gathered her into his arms. It wasn't the reaction she expected from him, but she wasn't going to complain. She burrowed deeper into his embrace, closing her eyes, and hoping that the moment could go on forever.

"I'm sorry," he whispered against her hair. "I've been telling you that you should say 'no' to Zoe, when I'm equally responsible for this."

She grimaced. So she had said something last night that she didn't remember.

"I haven't been very fair to you."

"It's just the lying that bothers me," she said. "There's no one I'd rather fake date than you."

He laughed.

She thought he might say something else, but then the moment passed.

"I'm going to go get ready," she told him, pulling herself away. She hesitated, before she quickly pressed her lips against his cheek. "Thank you for taking care of me."

He shook his head. "It was nothing. I'm glad you came to me."

She smiled and squeezed his hands.

"I'll see you later."

"See you later."

<hr>

HOLLY LIFTED the camera and snapped a few photos in rapid-succession as one of the employees at the bridal salon pinned the veil to Zoe's hair. She looked perfect, better than on the original fittings.

Before she left the shop, she knew that Zoe would expect her to try on the dress again, but after last night, Holly wasn't feeling anywhere near as generous. She would try it on, but she doubted she would wear it. Even with the hem taken up, she didn't have shoes to wear with it and it wouldn't be comfortable trying to move around and stay out of people's way.

Everything Zoe had said last night felt like it was hanging over her head. Holly just kept waiting for the other shoe to drop and it was making her feel sick.

"You're making me nervous," Sierra whispered.

Holly abruptly stopped tapping her leg.

"What's wrong with you?"

"Nothing."

Sierra stared.

"Okay, last night, Zoe said something that bothered me."

Sierra nodded.

"She said that it was basically you or me and she chose you."

"What?" Sierra hissed a little too loudly.

Amber glanced at them, but Sierra waved her hand.

Sierra plastered her sweetest smile on her face. "Zoe? Are you good on pictures for now? I think it's time for Holly to go try on her dress."

Zoe grinned brightly, hopping slightly on the pedestal. "Yes, of course. You should definitely do that."

Holly nodded slowly but fished the lens cap out from her pocket and let Sierra guide her to one of the fitting rooms.

"Okay, finish the story."

"What's there to finish?" Holly asked as she passed her camera off to Sierra and sat down to take off her boots. "She said that on the way up to her room and then slammed the door in my face when I told her I was tired."

"And you haven't talked at all since?"

"About what? I'm not going to beg her to be my friend."

Sierra shook her head but otherwise didn't comment. She waited for Holly to shuffle the dress over her head. The dress was shorter this time, but no less delicate or impractical. There was no way she would be able to work in this dress.

"I think I figured out the real reason you're not a bridesmaid," Sierra said. "She didn't want you to upstage her in the dress she picked out for you."

"It's not—"

"It really is. Look."

Holly did.

It didn't look any different than the last time, but Sierra was right that the color was better suited to Holly than it was for Lauren. The dress wasn't terrible either. If Holly hadn't been so annoyed with Zoe, she would have admitted that the style was something she would have picked out.

"Is she even paying you to photograph all this?" Sierra asked.

Holly turned. "Nope."

"Then there's nothing that says you have to wear this dress tomorrow."

"She paid for it. These dresses... I know they're not cheap..."

"They're not, but that doesn't mean you have to wear it. You're not part of the bridal party."

Sierra was right. She wasn't part of the bridal party and had no obligation to wear it, but after last night, she was so tired of it all. She didn't want to fight. She just wanted to get through the wedding and get on with her life. Starting a fight with Zoe over a dress was not the way to move forward.

"I just want to survive today. Let me worry about tomorrow later."

Sierra squeezed her hand, before her smile turned mischievous. "So Zach came to pick up your purse. And since I had your room key, you certainly spent the night somewhere..."

Holly rolled her eyes.

"Did anything exciting happen?"

"All the booze made me pass out?"

Sierra pouted. "That's nowhere near as fun. Let me live vicariously through you. You might be the only one here with a functional relationship."

Holly laughed. "What about Dennis and Sharon?"

Sierra waved a hand. "Please. Everyone knows old people don't count."

Holly shook her head as she laughed.

"I'm pretty sure that's not true."

The two of them walked out of the fitting room. Holly decided it was best to let Zoe gush about the great choice she made and to just smile and nod when appropriate. It was better than starting a fight.

Chapter Fourteen

HOLLY HATED how dark it was in the restaurant for the rehearsal dinner. It wouldn't be so bad, if Zoe hadn't asked already that Holly shut off her flash. Adjusting down for the lighting meant that she had to stay very still, and she knew she would have the same issue tomorrow at the wedding.

The rehearsal had gone without a hitch, even if Zoe and Ethan had been a bit cold to each other at the time.

The seating was similar to the welcome dinner. Zach and Holly glanced at each other from across the table and Sierra shook her head.

Holly's phone buzzed and she glance down.

SIERRA

Do you want to just switch?

HOLLY

And risk her wrath? No thanks.

SIERRA

It could be worse

You could be sitting next to Amber

Holly fought the smile that threatened to overtake her face at

Sierra's last message. She didn't want to make trouble at the wedding. Even if Zoe had been a terrible friend, there was no point in stooping to that same level. Holly would be a good guest and a good photographer. She would give Zoe exactly what she asked for with the pictures.

That evening, after the dinner was over and everyone said goodnight, Holly sat down at the table in her room with her laptop. She pulled out her card case and plugged the first SD card into the computer. With a few clicks, everything began to download onto her hard drive. She would edit them and copy them over for Zoe after she got back, but it didn't hurt to begin looking at them now.

She frowned as one of the photos flashed by. She hadn't seen it the other night, but Sierra must have taken it when she had been dancing with Zach at the welcome dinner. The next photo in the series was from when Holly had laid her head on Zach's shoulder.

She smiled as she saw it and dragged it onto her desktop. That picture was for her.

"WHAT ARE YOU WEARING?" Sierra asked as Holly stepped in the elevator the next morning. She looked and sounded far more awake than she had any right to be, despite the fact that she was wearing sweatpants to go downstairs.

Holly gave a small, slow twirl. The navy blue dress was one of her favorites. With an A-line cut, long sleeves, and pockets, it was one of the most versatile pieces she owned and she had gotten so much use out of it. She had warm leather boots for during the day and she would switch them later at the church for more appropriate pumps. Her coat lay over the handle of her camera bag which fortunately was on wheels. She kept imagining disaster after disaster where she tipped over and broke everything.

She had cut her nails neatly and cleaned off the last of the polish first thing this morning. There was no point in getting a manicure if she wasn't planning to be a bridesmaid.

"How scandalous. I love it."

"Oh, hush you."

Sierra snorted.

"But seriously, I'm surprised you decided not to wear it."

Holly had decided not to before, but Zoe's words the other night and her discussion with Sierra yesterday had clinched her decision. It may have been Zoe's wedding, but she wasn't going to feel like a charity case the whole day.

She wasn't going to say that to Sierra and risk Zoe accidentally hearing it. Instead, she said, "This is easier to take pictures in."

The elevator dinged and the doors slid open. The two of them stepped out. They were all getting ready together and Zoe had asked for pictures of them getting their hair and makeup done.

It would be a long time before Holly worked another wedding. Dealing with the bride's whims was just too much, and for what had to be the thousandth time this trip, she kicked herself for not just saying 'no' in the first place. If she could have just shown up the day of the wedding as a guest, her friendship with Zoe would still be preserved and her relationship with Zach unchanged. On the other hand, a part of her was glad that this was happening. Perhaps she would finally be able to close the door to the missed possibilities and move on from him.

Looking back, every relationship she had was probably overshadowed by 'what if it was Zach' so getting this out of her system was probably better for her long-term, even if it would hurt when it was over.

The morning passed in a rush of activity and it took until the bridesmaids were getting dressed for Zoe to realize that Holly was already clothed in what she intended to wear to the wedding. While she knew it was coming, she had not been looking forward to that confrontation.

"Why aren't you getting dressed?"

Holly blinked in mock confusion. "I am dressed."

Zoe shook her head, motioning to the rack with her bridal gown that was waiting for her hair to be finished. The stylist shot Holly a look like it was *her* fault.

"Not that. The dress I got you."

"It's a lovely dress, but I can't move well in that," Holly said softly. "I'll rip it trying to take pictures.

Zoe crossed her arms. "It's my wedding. Shouldn't what I say go?"

"I'm not a bridesmaid. And you're not paying me to be here."

She kept the same even, calm tone she had before. She wasn't trying to upset Zoe, though that would happen regardless.

Holly had put up with wearing some crazy outfits to blend in at a wedding, especially the themed weddings. But the clients usually paid handsomely for that and Holly would gladly wear a medieval gown or wizards' robes or a sci-fi space pilot's outfit when she was being paid.

And it helped that Holly usually chose her clients. Photographing this wedding had always been a favor, and her patience for that favor had run dry after the other night.

She saw Zoe's face go red before she turned back in her chair so the stylist could continue. Holly felt her stomach twist, but she refused to feel guilty. She was doing this all for free, donating her time, paying for her hotel room for over a week where she would have only paid for a couple of nights, had she just been attending as a guest. And with everything else, this was far past a labor of love.

She hated the way that Zoe was pouting, but she wasn't doing anything wrong and she would not let Zoe make her feel bad.

<hr>

THE CEREMONY WAS BEAUTIFUL. Zoe really had committed to the whole winter theme, with white flowers and white bows everywhere. She looked lovely in her wedding dress and the brides-maids all looked very pretty in their matching gowns. Zach looked good in his suit and she had a hard time remembering to focus on the bride and groom and not keep looking at the handsome groomsman.

Holly knew how to tuck herself away so it never ruined the view of the guests and so it didn't take the bride and groom out of the moment. Years of experience and practice taught her how to make herself invisible.

"You may now kiss the bride," the priest said and Holly snapped several pictures of the bride and groom. The first kiss was always the moment that felt easiest to miss. The first wedding she worked, when she was still very new and green, she missed the kiss. It was fortunate that her boss got the shot, but it wasn't a mistake she ever made again.

Zoe and Ethan walked out, hand in hand. Holly made sure to keep taking pictures of them until they got into the car and left. The bridal party followed and Holly climbed into the limo with them to go back to the hotel where the reception was.

Weirdly, Amber kept staring across the limo at Holly. The feeling of being watched made her uncomfortable and she reached out to Zach, gripping his hand tightly. He smiled down at her and she wanted to crawl behind him and hide until Amber forgot she was there.

"A few more hours," Zach murmured against her ear.

"Just a few."

She was counting them down.

***

DESPITE THE FACT that Zach was technically Holly's date, he had to walk Sierra into the reception. Sierra had shot her an apologetic look, but really it was better that it was Sierra walking him than Amber. Amber had plastered herself to Aaron's arm, and Holly thought the two of them were well-suited for each other.

Zoe and Ethan's grand entrance was quickly followed by their first dance, as well as the dances with their parents. By the time dinner was served, the batteries in Holly's camera were blinking. She was impressed with how long they lasted through the day.

In a fit of spitefulness, Zoe had left the original seating arrangements for the dinner, so Zach was with the bridal party between Sierra and Lauren and Holly was stuck at the table with the single relatives, Great Aunt Victoria and cousin Noah, among others that she hadn't met. The table was so far towards the back that it was clear they had only been invited because they were family and not because they were actually wanted. It felt petty.

"Sit down and eat," Aunt Victoria said as Holly tried to stand for at least the tenth time that night. Being at the back table did not make it easy to get decent photos, though she was quickly reaching the point where she was ready to give up. "It's not like you're going to get anything beyond them chewing and yakking."

On the other side of her, Noah snorted.

Holly let out a breath. "You're right."

She sat down in the chair and set the camera on the table. It was more important to eat than it was to get pictures of Zoe eating.

She was barely through her plate when a hand touched her shoulder. Holly looked up.

"Dance with me," Zach said.

She let him lead her to the dance floor and let him pull her into his arms. The way they fit together did nothing for her heart beating rapidly. It was going to be impossible to forget him after this. For someone faking it, why did he have to be so romantic about it?

"Really?"

Amber stood at the center of the floor, her hands on her hips as she glared at them.

"What?"

"How far do you two plan on going for attention?"

Holly blinked. All things considered, it was Amber making the scene, not them.

"What's going on?" Ethan asked as he pulled away from Zoe.

His bride looked less than impressed by that, glaring fiercely at everyone in the vicinity.

"I overheard them the other day," Amber said. "This whole thing has been an elaborate con."

"What has?" Zoe asked. Her eyes narrowed as she looked between the three of them.

"Them. Their relationship. They're faking it. They've been lying to everyone this whole time."

"If we were faking, would I do this?" Zach asked before he pulled Holly into a kiss.

It was everything she dreamed it would be when she had spent hours imagining what it would be like to kiss him. The reality was so much better.

Except for the fact that Amber was right. They were faking it.

"I don't know," Sierra said as loudly as Amber. "That looks pretty real to me."

Their stares didn't stop Zach from tangling his fingers in her hair and deepening the kiss. If anything, it encouraged him to go continue. And Holly wanted him to continue. She just wasn't sure her heart could take it.

Chapter Fifteen

AFTER THE KISS, it was amazing how quickly everyone decided that Amber had to be lying to get attention. She had sulked back to Aaron and left Holly and Zach in the middle of the floor. Leaving now would only draw unwanted eyes to them.

Her lips felt warm to the touch and it made her want to blush, but she refused to keep touching her mouth, on the off chance she might key someone in to the fact that Zach had never kissed her before.

"We should talk," Zach whispered into her ear as they swayed on the dance floor. "Not here. Once we get back upstairs."

Those words set her heart pounding and her stomach in knots, but not in a good way. Those famous last words of any relationship. From the beginning, she had worried that this would ruin their friendship, and now, it seemed that her worries had come to pass. She felt like she was going to be sick, but she refused to let the others in the room see. Instead, she would savor the moment and lock it away to cherish in the future.

The music changed suddenly and Holly looked up. The knot in her stomach tightened. She had been to far too many weddings and knew exactly what that meant.

"Alright, all you singles," she heard the DJ say. "It's time for the bouquet toss. Head to the center of the dance floor."

Zoe moved away from Ethan, up to the front by the DJ's booth. She wore a smile that seemed fake to Holly. She should be getting a picture of this, right? She should go get her camera from where she left it with Aunt Victoria and take photos of the toss and whoever caught it.

She didn't want to move. She found herself so reluctant to leave Zach's arms. It had to mean something that he hadn't let go yet, right? Perhaps it was just wishful thinking.

"Come on," Sierra said, taking her hand, before she looked at Zach. "You can have her back after."

Sierra pulled her into the middle before Holly could even think about arguing. Her palms felt sweaty and she could only hope that Sierra didn't notice.

Perhaps, if Holly was lucky, she would just dismiss it due to the room being so warm. It certainly felt warm. She wished she had worn a short sleeve dress, but being hot had never been an issue before.

It's the nerves, a voice in the back of her mind whispered.

She glanced back to where Zach had been, but he was no longer there. Where had he gone? Had he taken the chance to escape? No, he wanted to talk, so he wouldn't just leave, would he?

Some part of her was aware of Zoe speaking, but for the life of her, she didn't know what was being said. She could only hope that the videographer caught it all, though she wasn't sure she would ever watch it, not unless someone told her that something important had been said.

And then Zoe turned around. The others pushed and shoved, but Holly felt too ill to even look up into the air for where the bouquet was coming.

"Here!" others surrounding her called. At all of the weddings she had been to, Holly had never seen the bouquet go to where it was called. She had never participated in one before and wasn't sure she really wanted to be participating in one now.

"Look up!" Sierra shouted. It was all the more warning she had to lift her hands in the air. Something connected with her hand and she closed her fingers around it.

The bouquet. She stared down at it, feeling more than a little shocked. She had actually caught the bouquet.

A flash came from the corner of her eye.

"Holly!" someone called.

Holly blinked and looked in the direction of the voice. Zach held Holly's camera to his face and he was smiling. For a minute, the knot eased and she found herself grinning at him from across the room. The camera flashed again and it was worth it to blink away the spots behind her eyes.

It had been years since she was on that side of the camera for a wedding. She had to have been a teenager the last time. She certainly had never caught the bouquet before.

"Congratulations," someone to her right said.

Sierra nudged Holly's ribs with her elbow. "You know what that means, don't you?"

The sick feeling returned in force and she nearly dropped the bouquet. If she did that, everyone would wonder why and she would be forced to explain.

She couldn't explain to them. She didn't *want* to explain it to them.

"I'm just teasing," Sierra said.

"I know." She forced a smile on her face. "It's just been a long day."

"Tell me about it."

Sierra eyed Zoe and Ethan across the room where they were putting their coats on and people were beginning to line up to see them off. Zach appeared at Holly's side, camera in hand.

He smiled at her and Holly cursed her traitorous heart.

"I'll trade you."

Wordlessly, she held the bouquet out to him and took the camera from him. One last thing, and then she could go back upstairs and end the day. Maybe Zach would forget he wanted to talk to her and they could just pretend the entire week had never happened. From the other side of a computer screen, it wouldn't be so hard to do.

Like with everything else at the wedding, it seemed that Zoe had pulled out all of the stops. Rather than a car, a nice warm enclosed car to drive through the dark and snowy night, a white horse-drawn carriage waited for them.

"Wow," Holly muttered under her breath.

Beside her, Zach chuckled.

"What? You don't want horses at your wedding?"

"Not really," she answered without thinking. If she thought too much about him, she wouldn't pay attention to what she was doing and would miss the shot. She didn't want to miss the last few moments of the night.

It was only when Zoe and Ethan were in the carriage and the carriage had pulled out of sight that she lowered the camera. Through it all, Zach stayed close to her, acting as a human barrier to keep people from bumping into her.

She would miss the easy camaraderie and the way they worked together. The way he knew exactly what she had needed without her ever saying. She would miss so much about him.

Despite the cold, Holly almost wished that the reception had been held somewhere else. They could have had a long moonlit stroll back to the hotel before he inevitably broke her heart. She just wanted to savor what they had for a little bit longer, before it was gone forever.

She hated the hope she felt bubbling up when Zach offered her his hand.

"Heading out, lovebirds?" Sierra teased.

The word 'lovebirds' made her want to scream. Instead, she smiled and said, "Yeah, long day and all."

Zach nodded.

Sierra wrapped her arms around them, gathering them both up in one group hug. "Well, I probably won't see you in the morning before my flight. So Merry Christmas, both of you."

"Merry Christmas." Zach gave her a squeeze and then pulled away.

Holly lingered just a bit longer. She was a coward, trying her hardest to delay the inevitable, for all the good it would do. She wasn't looking forward to things being weird between them for Christmas at her parents.

"Don't be a stranger," Sierra whispered in her ear. "Keep in touch. I've missed you."

"The phone works both ways."

Sierra laughed, and Holly pulled away.

"Merry Christmas, and safe travels."

<h1 style="text-align:center">Chapter Sixteen</h1>

WHEN THE DOOR to the elevator opened, Holly no longer felt calm. It was just a miracle that Zach didn't see what a nervous mess she was. Or perhaps he had, and he had kindly chosen to ignore it. Holly wasn't sure which option was better.

Zach led her down the hall to his room and she let him, the suitcase with her camera equipment rolling awkwardly behind her. It was better this way. She could leave after, take a shower, and have a nice long cry in the privacy of her own room, and she wouldn't even have to worry about kicking him out. It was practically a win-win scenario, if it didn't feel so much like she was about to lose everything.

"I shouldn't have said that earlier," Zach started when he closed the room door behind them. "It was stupid to say it like that and I realized it as soon as I did."

Holly shrugged, the gesture half-hearted at best.

"I didn't mean to ruin your night."

"You didn't." At least, her night had already been a mess long before he uttered those infamous words.

He let out a breath and ran his fingers through his hair. "I don't know where to start."

Holly stared at him.

"I had it all planned out, ready to say earlier. It seemed so easy, and now..."

He let out a huff.

"The beginning is always a good place."

He laughed, but the sound was hallow and bitter and made Holly want to flinch. She wouldn't though. She never wanted him to think she was afraid of him.

"I'm just..." He frowned. "I knew."

She blinked.

"I knew about your crush back then. In high school. Zoe told me, well, screamed it at me once in the middle of a fight."

She flinched. He might as well have slapped her.

"I wanted to tell you at the time, but she swore me to secrecy and then you moved and I don't know." He shook his head. "I didn't want to mess things up between us. I thought if we talked more, that it would happen naturally if it was meant to be."

She thought about when he had first written to her. It had been the middle of the night and he had said he was trying to text his roommate. But Holly had still been awake and they spent the entire night texting back and forth. She fell asleep during her 8 a.m. lecture, but it had been worth it. The next time he texted, it hadn't been an accident.

He seemed almost sheepish about the whole thing.

Her heart hammered in her chest. She hated feeling so hopeful, but she couldn't help it. "So it wasn't that you didn't feel that way?"

He laughed. "Holly, I have turned down dates and canceled plans not to break our weekly movie watch parties. It's definitely not that."

She blushed. He held his arms open and she stepped into his embrace. He always gave the best hugs. He was just tall enough that she felt protected and secure, but the perfect height for her to lay her head against his shoulder and close her eyes. She felt him turn slightly and press his lips to her head.

"I haven't been pretending," he whispered against her hair.

"And I wouldn't mind if this was real. I love you and I want this to be real."

"And how would it work? We live thousands of miles away from each."

"We don't have to."

She pulled back and stared at him.

"I got offered a job near you. I was planning to take it." He smiled. "Supposedly, it's less crazy hours and less flying all over the world."

"But do you want that?"

She didn't want him to feel like she had held him back.

He nodded. "It's been something I've wanted for a while now. I talked to Sierra the other day and she mentioned a place near you that she knows is hiring. I have an interview with them in the new year." He hesitated, his smile a little less sure. "If you don't want me to take it, I won't."

Holly laughed and reached for him, pulling his face to her height so she could kiss him. She could tell that she had shocked him and it took a moment for him to respond. His arms wrapped around her tighter, pulling her flush to him.

"I love you," she whispered when they broke apart. "I've loved you for a long time."

He stared at her. "Marry me."

"What? We haven't even dated. We don't know if we can live in the same state long-term."

He tilted his head slightly. "Is that a 'no'?"

Holly froze. "No. I mean, no, it's not a no. Yes, I'll marry you, but not right now."

He grinned, and it felt like the sun was peeking through the clouds. He dipped down and kissed her quickly before he let go long enough to reach into his pocket and fish something out.

He took her hand in his and slid the ring on it.

"Wait," she realized. "This is your grandmother's ring. Is this what you got from your dad the other day?"

"Everyone knew that I was in love with you before I knew it myself."

He said the words so simply, so matter of factly, that she couldn't help but stare. She had to be dreaming. Any second now, she would wake up and it would have all been some beautiful dream.

"We can do a long engagement. We can see about all the things we talked about. But I just know that I love you and I don't want to live without you anymore."

Holly grinned and let him kiss her again.

The End.

About the Author

Named for the famous fictional mystery writer Jessica Fletcher, Jessica Baker picked up a pen when she was in elementary school and never set it down.

Jessica lives in sunny Central Florida and is a member of the National Sisters in Crime. When she's not writing, she works at a university and freelances as a camera assistant in film which provides plenty of inspiration for her stories.

To learn more about Jessica and her books, visit her at www. jessicabakerauthor.com and for the latest information, subscribe to her newsletters.

9 781960 102072